NEVER SAY NO
TO A CAFFARELLI

NEVER SAY NO TO A CAFFARELLI

BY

MELANIE MILBURNE

Published in Great Britain 2013
by Mills & Boon, an imprint of Harlequin (UK) Limited.
Large Print edition 2014
Harlequin (UK) Limited, Eton House,
18-24 Paradise Road, Richmond, Surrey, TW9 1SR

ISBN: 978 0 263 24008 5

Harlequin (UK) Limited's policy is to use papers that are natural, renewable and recyclable products and made from wood grown in sustainable forests. The logging and manufacturing processes conform to the legal environmental regulations of the country of origin.

Printed and bound in Great Britain
by CPI Antony Rowe, Chippenham, Wiltshire

To Sharon Kendrick,
a Harlequin Mills & Boon sister
and dear friend. XXX

CHAPTER ONE

'WHAT DO YOU MEAN, she won't sell?' Raffaele Caffarelli frowned at his London-based secretary.

Margaret Irvine turned her palms over in a 'don't blame me' gesture. 'Miss Silverton flatly refused your offer.'

'Then make her a bigger one.'

'I did. She refused that too.'

Rafe drummed his fingers on the desk for a moment. He hadn't been expecting a hiccup like this at this stage. Everything had gone smoothly up until now. He'd had no trouble acquiring the stately English countryside manor and surrounding land in Oxfordshire for a bargain price. But the dower house was on a separate title—a minor problem, or so he'd been led to believe by his business manager, as well as the estate agent. The agent had assured him it would be easy enough to acquire the dower house so that the Dalrymple

Estate could be whole once more; all he would have to do was to offer well above the market value. Rafe had been generous in his offer. Like the rest of the estate, the place was run down and badly needed a makeover, and he had the money needed to bring it back to its former glory and turn it into a masterpiece of English style and decadence. What was the woman thinking? How could she be in her right mind to turn down an offer as good as his?

He *wasn't* going to give up on this. He had seen the property listed online and got his business manager, James—who was going to be fired if this didn't get sorted out soon—to secure it for him.

Failure was not a word anyone would dare to associate with the name Raffaele Caffarelli. He was not going to let a little hurdle like this get in the way of what he wanted. 'Do you think this Silverton woman's somehow found out it's me who's bought Dalrymple Manor?'

'Who knows?' Margaret shrugged. 'But I wouldn't have thought so. We've managed to keep the press away from this so far. James handled all the paperwork under cover and I made the offer to Miss Silverton via the agent, as you instructed. You don't know her personally, do you?'

'No, but I've met her type before.' Rafe curled his lip cynically. 'Once she gets a whiff that it's a wealthy developer after her house, she'll go for broke. She'll try and milk every penny she can out of me.' He let out a short sharp expletive. 'I *want* that property. I want *all* of that property.'

Margaret pushed a folder across the desk to him. 'I found some news clippings from the local village from a couple of years ago about the old man who owned the manor. It seems the late Lord Dalrymple had rather a soft spot for Poppy Silverton and her grandmother. Beatrice Silverton was the head housekeeper at the manor. Apparently she worked there for years and—'

'Gold-digger,' Rafe muttered.

'Who? The grandmother?'

He shoved his chair back and got to his feet. 'I want you to find out everything you can about this woman Polly. I want her—'

'Poppy. Her name is Poppy.'

Rafe rolled his eyes and continued. 'Poppy, then. I want her background, her boyfriends—even her bra size. Leave no stone unturned. I want it on my desk first thing Monday morning.'

Margaret's neatly pencilled eyebrows lifted but the rest of her expression remained in 'obedient secretary' mode. 'I'll get working on it right away.'

Rafe paced the floor as his secretary gathered a stack of documents to be filed from his desk. Maybe he should head down and have a little snoop around the village himself. He'd only seen the manor and the surrounding area from the photos James had emailed him. It wouldn't hurt to have a little reconnaissance trip of his own to size up the enemy, so to speak.

He snatched up his keys. 'I'm heading out of town for the weekend. Anything urgent, call me, otherwise I'll see you on Monday.'

'Who's the lucky girl this time?' Margaret gathered the bundle of paperwork against her chest. 'Is it still the Californian bikini-model or is she yesterday's news?'

He shrugged on his jacket. 'This may surprise

you, but I'm planning to spend this weekend on my own.' He stopped pulling down his left shirt cuff to glower at her. 'What's that look for?'

His secretary gave him a knowing smile.' You haven't spent a weekend on your own since I don't know when.'

'So?' He gave her another brooding frown. 'There's a first time for everything, isn't there?'

Poppy was bending over to clear table three when the door of her tearoom opened on Saturday afternoon. Even with her back to the door she knew it wasn't one of her regulars. The tinkling chime of the bell sounded completely different. She turned around with a welcoming smile, but it faltered for a moment as she encountered an open shirt-collar and a glimpse of a tanned masculine chest at the height she'd normally expect to see someone's face.

She tilted her head right back to meet a pair of brown eyes that were so intensely dark they looked almost black. The staggeringly handsome face with its late-in-the-day stubble seemed vaguely familiar. A movie star, perhaps? A celebrity of some sort? She flicked through her mental hard-drive but couldn't place him. 'Um, a table for…?'

'One.'

A table for one? Poppy mentally rolled her eyes. He didn't look the 'table for one' type. He looked the type who would have a veritable harem of adoring women trailing after him wherever he went.

Maybe he was a model, one of those men's aftershave ones—the ones that looked all designer stubbly, masculine and bad-boy broody in those glossy magazine advertisements.

But who went to old-world tearooms on their own? That was what the coffee chain stores were for—somewhere to linger for hours over a macchiato and a muffin and mooch through a raft of the day's papers.

Poppy's stomach suddenly dropped in alarm. *Was he a food critic?* Oh, dear God! Was she about to be savaged in some nasty little culinary blog that would suddenly go viral and ruin everything for her? She was struggling to keep afloat as it was. Things had been deadly quiet since that swanky new restaurant—which she couldn't even name or think of without wanting to throw up—opened in the next village. The down-turn in the economy meant people weren't treating themselves to the luxury of high tea any more.

They saved their pennies and went out to dinner instead—*at her ex-boyfriend's restaurant.*

Poppy studied the handsome stranger covertly as she led him to table four. 'How about over here?' She pulled out a chair as she tried to place the faint trace of an accent. French? Italian? A bit of both, perhaps? 'You get a lovely view of Dalrymple Manor and the maze in the distance.'

He gave the view a cursory glance before turning back to her. Poppy felt a little shock like volts of electricity shooting through her body when that dark-as-night gaze meshed with hers. God, how gorgeous was his mouth! So masculine and firm with that sinfully sensual, fuller lower lip. Why on earth didn't he sit down? She would have a crick in her neck for the rest of the day.

'Is that some sort of tourist attraction?' he asked. 'It looks like something out of a Jane Austen novel.'

She gave him a wry look. 'It's the *only* tourist attraction, not that it's open to the public or anything.'

'It looks like a rather grand place.'

'It's a fabulous place.' Poppy released a wistful little sigh. 'I spent most of my childhood there.'

A dark brow arched up in a vaguely interested manner. 'Oh really?'

'My grandmother used to be the housekeeper for Lord Dalrymple. She started at the manor when she was fifteen and stayed until the day he died. She never once thought of getting another job. You don't get loyalty like that any more, do you?'

'Indeed you don't.'

'She passed away within six months of him.' Poppy sighed again. 'The doctors said it was an aneurysm, but personally I think she didn't know what to do with herself once he'd gone.'

'So who lives there now?'

'No one at the moment,' she said. 'It's been vacant for over a year while the probate was sorted out on Lord Dalrymple's will. There's a new owner but no one knows who it is or what they plan to do with the place. We're all dreading the thought that it's been sold to some crazy, money-hungry developer with no taste. Another part of our local history will be lost for ever under some ghastly construction called—' she put her fingers up to signify quotation marks '—modern architecture.'

'Aren't there laws to prevent that from happening?'

'Yes, well, some people with loads of money think they're above the law.' Poppy gave a disdainful, rolling flicker of her eyes. 'The more money they have, the more power they seem to expect to wield. It makes my blood boil. Dalrymple Manor needs to be a family home again, not some sort of playboy party-palace.'

'It looks rather a large property for the average family of today,' he observed. 'There must be three storeys at least.'

'Four,' she said. 'Five, if you count the cellar. But it needs a family. It's been crying out for one ever since Lord Dalrymple's wife died in childbirth all those years ago.'

'I take it he didn't marry again?'

'Clara was the love of his life and once she died that was that,' she said. 'He didn't even look at another woman. You don't get that sort of commitment these days, do you?'

'Indeed you don't.'

Poppy handed him a menu to bridge the little silence that had ensued. Why was she talking about loyalty and commitment to a perfect stranger? Chloe, her assistant, was right: maybe she did need to get out more. Oliver's betrayal had made her horribly cynical. He had wooed her and then exploited her in the worst way imaginable. He hadn't wanted *her;* he'd used her knowledge and expertise to set up a rival business. How gullible she had been to fall for it! She still shuddered to think about how close she had come to sleeping with him. 'Um, we have a special cake of the day. It's a ginger sponge with raspberry jam and cream.'

The dark-haired man ignored the menu and sat down. 'Just coffee.'

Poppy blinked. She had forty varieties of specialty teas and he wanted *coffee?* 'Oh…right. What sort? We have cappuccino, latte—'

'Double-shot espresso. Black, no sugar.'

Would it hurt you to crack a smile? What was it with some men? And who the hell went to a *tearoom* to drink *coffee?*

There was something about him that made Poppy feel prickly and defensive. She couldn't help feeling he was mocking her behind those dark, unreadable eyes. Was it her Edwardian dress and frilly apron? Was it her red-gold curly hair bunched up under her little mobcap? Did he think she was a little bit behind the times? That was the whole point of Poppy's Teas—it was an old-world experience, a chance to leave the 'rush, rush, rush' pace of the modern world behind while you enjoyed a good old-fashioned cup of tea and home baking just like your great-great granny used to make.

'Coming right up.' Poppy swung away, carried her tray back to the kitchen and put it down on the counter top with a little rattle of china cups.

Chloe looked up from where she was sandwiching some melting moments with butter-cream. 'What's wrong? You look a little flushed.' She narrowed her gaze to slits. 'Don't tell me that two-timing jerk Oliver has come in with his slutty new girlfriend just to rub salt in the wound. When I think of the way he pinched all of those wonderful recipes of yours to pass them off as his own creation I want to cut off his you-know-whats and serve them as an entrée in his totally rubbish restaurant.'

'No.' Poppy frowned as she unloaded the tray. 'It's just some guy I have a feeling I've seen somewhere before…'

Chloe put down her knife and tiptoed over to peek through the glass of the swing door. 'Oh. My. God.' She turned back to Poppy with wide eyes. 'It's one of the Three Rs.'

Poppy screwed up her face. 'One of the what?'

'The Caffarelli brothers,' Chloe said in a hushed voice. 'There's three of them. Raffaele, Raoul and Remy. Rafe is the oldest. They're French-Italian squillionaires. The seriously-silver-spoon set: private jets, fast cars and even faster women.'

Poppy gave her head a little toss as she went to the coffee machine. 'Well, for all that money it certainly hasn't taught him any manners. He didn't even say please or thank you.' She gave the knob of the machine a savage little twist. 'Nor did he smile.'

Chloe peeked through the glass panel again. 'Maybe you don't have to be nice to horribly common people like us when you're filthy rich.'

'My gran used to say you can tell a lot about a person by the way they respect people they don't *have* to respect,' Poppy said. 'Lord Dalrymple was a shining example of it. He treated everyone the same. It didn't matter if they were a cleaner or a corporate king.'

Chloe came back to the melting moments and picked up her butter-cream knife. 'I wonder what he's doing in our little backwater village? We're not exactly on the tourist trail these days. The new motorway took care of that.'

Poppy's hand froze on the espresso machine. 'It's *him*.'

'Him?'

'He's the new owner of Dalrymple Manor.' Poppy ground her teeth as she faced her assistant. 'He's the one who wants to turf me out of my home. I knew there was something funny about that woman who came by the other day with that pushy agent. I bet *he* sent her to do his dirty work for him.'

'Uh-oh…' Chloe winced. 'I know what this means.'

Poppy straightened her shoulders and pasted a plastic-looking smile on her face. 'You're right.' She picked up the steaming double-shot espresso as she headed towards the door leading out to the tearoom. '*This means war.*'

Rafe cast an eye around the quaint tearoom. It was like stepping back in time. It gave him a sort of spooky time-warp sensation where he almost expected a First World War soldier to walk in the door with an elegantly dressed lady on his arm. The delicious smell of home baking filled the air. Fresh cottage flowers were on the dainty tables—sweet peas, forget-me-nots and columbines—and there were hand-embroidered linen napkins on each place setting. The teacups and plates were a colourful but mismatched collection of old china, no doubt sourced from antique stores all over the countryside.

It told him a lot about the owner-operator. He

presumed the flame-haired beauty who had served him was Poppy Silverton. She wasn't quite what he'd been expecting. He had pictured someone older, someone a little more hard-boiled, so to speak.

Poppy Silverton looked like she'd just stepped out of the pages of a children's fairy-tale book. She had a riot of red-gold curls stuffed—rather unwillingly, he suspected, given the tendrils that had escaped around her face—under a maid's mobcap; brown eyes the colour of toffee, and a rosy mouth that looked as soft and plump as red velvet cushions. Her skin was creamy and unlined, with just the tiniest sprinkling of freckles over the bridge of her nose that looked like a dusting of nutmeg over a baked custard. She was a mix between Cinderella and Tinkerbell.

Cute—but not his type, of course.

The swing door to the kitchen opened and out she came bearing a steaming cup of coffee. She had a smile on her face that didn't show her teeth or quite reach her eyes. 'Your coffee, *sir.*'

Rafe caught a faint trace of her flowery perfume as she bent down to place his coffee on the table. He couldn't quite place the fragrance…lily of the valley or was it freesia? 'Thank you.'

She straightened and fixed him with a direct stare. 'Are you sure you wouldn't like a piece of cake? We have other varieties, or cookies if you're not a cake man.'

'I don't have a sweet tooth.'

She pursed her full mouth for a brief moment, as if she took his savoury preference as a personal slight. 'We have sandwiches. Our ribbon ones are our specialty.'

'The coffee is all I want.' He picked up his cup and gave her one of his formal smiles. 'Thank you.'

She leaned over to pick up a fallen petal from one of the columbines and he got another whiff of her intriguing scent and a rather spectacular view of her small but delightful cleavage. She had a neat, ballerina-like figure, curves in all the right places and a waist he was almost certain he could have spanned with his hands. He could sense she was hovering, delaying the moment when she would have to go back to the kitchen.

Had she guessed who he was? She hadn't

shown any sign of the instant flash of recognition he usually got. She had looked at him quizzically, as if trying to place him, when he'd first come in but he had seen confusion rather than confirmation in her gaze. It was rather comforting to think that not *everyone* in Britain had heard about his latest relationship disaster. He didn't set out deliberately to hurt any of his lovers, but in this day and age a woman scorned was a woman well armed with the weapons of mass destruction more commonly known as social media.

Poppy Silverton moved over to one of the other tables and straightened the already perfectly straight napkins.

Rafe couldn't take his eyes off her. She drew him like a magnet. She was so other-worldly, so intriguing, he felt almost spellbound.

Get a grip. You're here to win this, not be beguiled by a woman who's probably as streetwise as the next. Don't let that innocent bow of a mouth or those big Bambi eyes fool you.

'Are you usually this busy?' he asked.

She turned and faced him again but her tight expression told him she didn't appreciate his dry sense of humour. 'We had a very busy morning. One of the busiest we've ever had. We were run off our feet. It was bedlam.... I had to make a second batch of scones.'

Rafe knew she was lying. This tiny little village was so quiet even the church mice had packed up and left for somewhere more exciting. That was why he'd wanted the manor. It was the perfect place to build a luxury hotel for the rich and famous who wanted to secure their privacy. He took a measured sip of his coffee. It was much better than he'd been expecting. 'How long have you been running this place? I'm assuming you're the owner?'

'Two years.'

'Where were you before?'

She wiped an invisible crumb from the table next to his. 'I was sous chef at a restaurant in Soho. I decided I wanted to spend some time with my gran.'

Rafe suspected there was more to her career change than that. It would be interesting to see what his secretary managed to unearth about her.

He sat back and watched her for a moment. 'What about your parents? Do they live locally?'

Her face tightened and her shoulders went back in a bracing manner. 'I don't have parents. I haven't had since I was seven years old.'

'I'm sorry to hear that.' Rafe knew all about growing up without parents. When he was ten, his had died in a boating accident on the French Riviera. A grandparent had reared him, but he got the feeling that Poppy Silverton's grandmother had been nothing like his autocratic, overbearing grandfather Vittorio. 'Do you run this place by yourself?'

'I have another girl working for me. She's in the kitchen.' She gave him another rather pointed look. 'Are you just passing through the village or are you staying locally?'

He put his cup back down in the saucer with measured precision. 'I'm just passing through.'

'What brings you to these parts?'

Was it his imagination or had her caramel-brown eyes just flashed at him? 'I'm doing some research.'

'For?'

'For a project I'm working on.'

'What sort of project?'

Rafe picked up his cup again and surveyed her indolently for a moment. 'Do you give every customer the third degree as soon as they walk in the door?'

Her mouth flattened and her hands went into small fists by her sides. 'I *know* why you're here.'

He lazily arched a brow at her. 'I came in here for coffee.'

Her eyes flashed at him; there was no mistaking it this time. They were like twin bolts of lightning at they clashed with his. 'You did not. You came to scope out the territory. You came to size up the opposition. I *know* who you are.'

He gave her one of his disarming smiles, the sort of smile that had closed more business deals and opened more bedroom doors than he could count. 'I came here to make you an offer you can't refuse.' He leaned back in the chair; confident he would find her price and nail this in one fell swoop. 'How much do you want for the dower house?'

She eyeballed him. 'It's *not* for sale.'

Rafe felt a stirring of excitement in his blood. So, she was going to play hard to get, was she? He would enjoy getting her to capitulate. He thrived on challenges, the harder the better—the more satisfying.

Failure wasn't a word he allowed in his vocabulary.

He would win this.

He gave her a sizing-up look, taking in her flushed cheeks and glittering eyes. He knew what she was doing—ramping up the price to get as much as she could out of him.

So predictable.

'How much to get you to change your mind?'

Her eyes narrowed to hairpin-thin slits as she planted her hands on the table right in front of him so firmly his fine-bone china cup rattled in its saucer. 'Let's get something straight right from the get-go, Mr Caffarelli: you *can't* buy me.'

He took a leisurely glance at the delectable shadow between her breasts before he met her feisty gaze with his cool one. 'You misunderstand me, Miss Silverton. I don't want *you*. I just want your house.'

Her cheeks were bright red with angry defiance as she glared at him. 'You're *not* getting it.'

Rafe felt a quiver of primal, earthy lust rumble through his blood that set off a shivery sensation all the way to his groin. He couldn't remember the last time a woman had said no to him. It spoke to everything that was alpha in him. This was going to be much more fun that he'd thought.

He would *not* stop until he got that house, and her with it.

He rose to his feet and she jerked backwards as if he had just breathed a dragon's tongue of fire on her. 'But I will.' He laid a fifty-pound note on the table between them, locking his gaze with her fiery one. 'That's for the coffee. Keep the change.'

CHAPTER TWO

'GRRHH!' POPPY SHOVED the kitchen door open so hard it crashed back against the wall. 'I can't believe the gall of that man. He thought he could just waltz in here, wave a big fat wad of notes under my nose and I'd sell my house to him. How…how *arrogant* is that?'

Chloe's blue eyes were wider than the plates she'd been pretending to put away. 'What the hell happened out there? I thought you were going to punch him.'

Poppy glowered at her. 'He's the most detestable man I've ever met. I will *never* sell my house to him. Do you hear me? *Never*.'

'How much was he offering?'

Poppy scowled. 'What's that got to with anything? It wouldn't matter if he offered me gazillions—I wouldn't take it.'

'Are you sure you're doing the right thing

here?' Chloe asked. 'I know your house has a lot of sentimental value because of living there with your gran and all, but your circumstances have changed. She wouldn't expect you to turn down a fortune just because of a few memories.'

'It's not just about the memories,' Poppy said. 'It's the only home I've ever known. Lord Dalrymple left it to Gran *and* me. I can't just sell it as if it's a piece of furniture I don't want.'

'Seriously, though, what about the bills?' Chloe asked with a worried little frown.

Poppy tried to ignore the gnawing panic that was eating away her stomach lining like caustic soda on satin. Worrying about how she was going to pay the next month's rent on the tearoom had kept her awake for three nights in a row. Her savings had taken a hit after paying for her gran's funeral, and she had been playing catch-up ever since. Bills kept coming through the post, one after the other. She'd had no idea owning your own home could be so expensive. And, if Oliver's rival restaurant hadn't impinged on things enough, one of her little rescue dogs, Pickles, had needed a cruciate ligament repair. The vet had charged her mate's rates but it had still made a sizable dent in her bank account. 'I've got things under control.'

Chloe looked doubtful. 'I wouldn't burn too many bridges just yet. Things have been pretty slow for spring. We only sold one Devonshire tea this morning. I'll have to freeze the scones.'

'No, don't do that,' Poppy said. 'I'll take them to Connie Burton. Her three boys will soon demolish them.'

'That's half your problem, you know,' Chloe said. 'You run this place like a charity instead of a business. You're too soft-hearted.'

Poppy ground her teeth as she started rummaging in the stationery drawer. 'I'm not accepting *his* charity.' She located an envelope and stuffed the change from the coffee into it. 'I'm handing his tip back to him as soon as I finish here.'

'He tipped you?'

'He *insulted* me.'

Chloe's expression was incredulous. 'By leaving you a fifty-pound note for an espresso? I reckon we could do with a few more customers like him.'

Poppy sealed the envelope as if it contained something toxic and deadly. 'You know what? I'm not going to wait until I finish work to give this to him. I'm going to take it to him right now. Be a honey and close up for me?'

'Is he staying at the manor?'

'I'm assuming so,' Poppy said. 'Where else would he stay? It's not as if we have any five-star hotels in the village.'

Chloe gave her a wry look. 'Not yet.'

Poppy set her mouth and snatched up her keys. 'If Mr Caffarelli thinks he's going to build one of his playboy mansions here, then it will be over my dead body.'

Rafe was in the formal sitting room inspecting some water damage near one of the windows when he saw Poppy Silverton come stomping up the long gravel driveway towards the manor. Her cloud of curly hair—now free of her cute little mobcap—was bouncing as she went, her hands were going like two metronome arms by her sides and in one hand she was carrying a white envelope.

He smiled.

So predictable.

He waited until she had knocked a couple of times before he opened the door. 'How delightful,' he drawled as he looked down at her flushed heart-shaped face and sparkling brown eyes. 'My very first visitor. Aren't I supposed to carry you over the threshold or something?'

She gave him a withering look. 'This is your change.' She shoved the envelope towards his chest.

Rafe ignored the envelope. 'You Brits really have a problem with tipping, don't you?'

Her pretty little mouth flattened. 'I'm not accepting anything from you.' She pushed the envelope towards him again. 'Here. Take it.'

He folded his arms across his chest and gave her a taunting smile. 'No.'

Her eyes pulsed and flashed with loathing. He wondered for a moment whether she was going to slap him. He found himself hoping she would, for it would mean he would have to stop her. The thought of putting his arms around her trim little body to restrain her was surprisingly and rather deliciously tempting.

She blew out a breath and, standing up on tiptoe, stashed the envelope into the breast pocket of his shirt. He felt the high voltage of her touch through the fine cotton layer of his shirt. She must have felt it too, for she tried to snatch her hand back as if his body had scorched her.

But she wasn't quick enough for him.

Rafe captured her hand, wrapping his fingers around her wrist where he could feel her pulse leaping. Her lithe but luscious little body was so close he felt the jut of one of her hipbones against his thigh. Desire roared through his veins like the backdraft from a deadly fire. He was erect within seconds; aching and throbbing with a lust so powerful it took every ounce of self-control he possessed to stop from pushing her up against the nearest wall to see how far he could go.

She sent him an icy glare and tugged against his hold, hissing at him like a cornered wild cat. 'Get your hands off me.'

Rafe kept her tethered to him with his fingers while he moved the pad of his thumb over the underside of her wrist in a stroking motion. 'You touched me first.'

Her eyes narrowed even further and she tugged again. 'Only because you wouldn't take your stupid money off me.'

He released her hand and watched as she rubbed at it furiously, as if trying to remove the sensation of his touch. 'It was a gift. That's what a tip is—a gesture of appreciation for outstanding service.'

She stopped rubbing at her wrist to glare at him again. 'You're making fun of me.'

'Why would I do that?' He gave her a guileless half-smile. 'It was a great cup of coffee.'

'You won't win this, you know.' She drilled him with her glittering gaze. 'I know you probably think I'm just an unworldly, unsophisticated country girl, but you have *no* idea how determined I can be.'

Rafe felt his skin prickle all over with delight at the challenge she was laying before him. It was like a shot of a powerful drug. It galvanised him. And as for unsophisticated and unworldly… Well, he would never admit it to his two younger brothers, but he was getting a little bored with the worldly women he associated with. Just lately he had started to feel a little restless. The casual affairs were satisfying on a physical level, but recently he'd walked away from each of them with an empty feeling that had lodged in a place deep inside him.

But, even more unsettling, a niggling little question had started keeping him awake until the early hours of the morning: *is this all there is?*

Maybe it was time to broaden his horizons. It would certainly be entertaining to bring Miss Poppy Silverton to heel. She was like a wild filly who hadn't met the right trainer. What would it take to have her eating out of his hand? His body gave another shudder of delight.

He could hardly wait.

'I think I should probably warn you at this point, Miss Silverton, that I'm no pushover. I play by the rules, but they're *my* rules.'

Her chin came up at that. 'I *detest* men like you. You think you're above everyone else with your flash cars and luxury villas in every country and yet another vacuous model or starlet hanging off your arm, simpering over every word that comes out of your silver-spooned mouth. But I bet there are times when you lie awake at night wondering if anyone loves you just for who you are as a person or whether it's just for your money.'

He curled his lip mockingly. 'You really have a thing about well-heeled men, don't you? Why is success such a big turn-off for you?'

She gave him a scoffing look. 'Success? Don't make me laugh. You inherited all your wealth. It's not *your* success, it's your family's. You're just riding on the wave of it, just like your party-boy, time-wasting brothers.'

Rafe thought of all the hard work he and his brothers had had to do to keep their family's wealth secure. Some unwise business dealings his grandfather had made a few years ago had jeopardised everything. Rafe had marshalled his brothers and as a team they had rebuilt their late father's empire. It had taken eighteen-hour days, working seven days a week for close to two and a half years to bring things back around, but they had done it. Thankfully, none of Vittorio's foolhardiness had ever been leaked to the press, but hardly a day went by without Rafe remembering how terrifyingly close they had been to losing everything. He, perhaps a little more than Raoul and Remy, felt the ongoing burden of responsibility, to the extent that he had earned the reputation in the corporate world of a being a rather ruthless, single-minded workaholic.

'You are very keen to express an opinion on matters of which you know nothing,' he said. 'Have you met either of my brothers?'

'No, and I don't want to. I'm sure they're just as detestable and loathsome as you.'

'Actually, they're vastly nicer than me.'

'Oh really?' She raised her brows in a cynical arc.

Rafe leaned indolently against the sandstone pillar, his arms folded loosely across his chest, one of his legs crossed over the other at the ankle. 'For instance, they would never leave a young lady standing out here on the steps without inviting her in for a drink.'

Her eyes narrowed in warning. 'Well, if you're thinking of asking me in, then don't bother wasting your breath.'

'I wasn't.'

Her expression faltered for a nanosecond but then she quickly recovered her pertness. 'I'm quite sure I'd be a novel change from the women you usually invite in for drinks.'

He swept his gaze over her lazily. 'Indeed you would. I've never had a redhead before.'

Her cheeks coloured and her mouth tightened. 'It's not red. It's auburn.'

'It's very beautiful.'

Her gaze flashed with venom. 'If you think flattery is going to work with me, then think again. I'm not going to sell my house to you no matter how many insincere compliments you conjure up.'

'Why are you so attached to the place?' Rafe asked. 'You could buy a much bigger place in a better location with the money I offered you.'

She gave him a hard little look. 'I don't expect someone like you to understand; you've probably lived in luxury homes all your life. The dower house is the first place I've ever been able to call home. I know it's not flash, and that it needs a bit of work here and there, but if I sold it would be like selling part of myself.'

'No one is asking you to sell yourself.'

Her brows arched up again. 'Are they not?'

Rafe held her gaze for several beats. 'My plans for the manor will go ahead with or without your cooperation. I understand the sentiments you expressed, but they have no place in what is at the end of the day a business decision. You would be committing financial suicide to reject the kind of offer I've made.'

Her posture was stiff and defensive, her eyes slitted in hatred. 'You know nothing of my financial affairs. You don't know *me*.'

'Then I will enjoy getting to know you.' He gave her a smouldering look. 'In every sense of the word.'

She swung away with her colour high and stomped back down the steps. Rafe watched her disappear into the distance with a smile on his face. One way or the other he was going to win this.

He would stake money on it.

Poppy was still fuming when she got back to her house. Her three little dogs—Chutney, Pickles and Relish—looked up at her with worried eyes as she stormed through the gate. 'Sorry, guys,' she said bending down to give them all a scratch behind the ears. 'I'm just so cross I can hardly stand it. What an arrogant man! Who does he think he is? As if I'd fall for someone like him. As if I'd even *think* about sleeping with him.'

Well, maybe it was OK to *think* about it a teeny weeny bit. There was no harm in that, was there? It wasn't as if she was going to act on it. She wasn't that type of girl. Which kind of explained why her ex-boyfriend was now shacked up with another woman.

Poppy knew it was ridiculously old-fashioned of her to have wanted to wait a while before she consummated her relationship with Oliver. It wasn't that she was a prude... Well, maybe a bit, given she'd been raised by her grandmother, who hadn't had sex in decades.

The trouble was she was a soppy romantic at heart. She wanted her first time to be special. She wanted it to be special for the man who shared it with her. She'd thought Oliver Kentridge was going to be that special man who would open up the world of sensuality to her, but he had betrayed her even before they'd been dating a couple of months.

Poppy couldn't say her heart had been broken, but it had definitely been heavily bruised. Men were such selfish creatures, or at least that was how it had seemed in her life so far. Her well-heeled but wild playboy father had deserted her mother as soon as she had told him she was pregnant. And then, to rub more salt in the wound, within weeks of Poppy's birth he had married a wealthy socialite who stood to inherit a fortune to prop up his own. Her mother had been devastated by being cast aside so heartlessly and, in a moment of impulsivity, no doubt fuelled by her hurt, had turned up at his high-society wedding with her 'child of scandal', as Poppy had been called. The press attention had only made her mother's suffering worse and horribly, excruciatingly public. Poppy had frighteningly clear memories from during her early years of running down back-alleys holding tightly to her mother's hand, trying to avoid the paparazzi. During that time her mother had been too proud to go to her own mother for help and support for fear of hearing the dreaded 'I told you so'.

Poppy still remembered that terrifying day when the grandmother she had never met came to collect her from the hospital where her mother had drawn her last breath after taking an overdose. Her gran had seemed a little formidable at first, but over time Poppy realised it was her way of coping with the grief of losing her only child, and her regret at not having stepped in sooner to help her daughter cope with the heartbreak and shame of being cast aside by a rich man who had only used her.

Her gran had done her best to give Poppy a happy childhood. Growing up on the Dalrymple Estate had been a mostly happy but rather lonely existence. Lord Dalrymple rarely entertained and there were no children living close by. But it had gradually become home to her, and she had loved spending time with her gran in the kitchen at the manor.

The decision to study hospitality had been born out of Poppy's desire to own and run her own tearoom in the village one day, so she could be close to her gran and all that was familiar. When she moved to London to do her training she felt like she was the odd one out in her peer group. She didn't have much of a taste for alcohol and she had no interest in casual flings or partying all night in nightclubs. She'd studied hard and managed to land a great job in a hip new restaurant in Soho, but it had all turned sour when her boss had made it clear he wanted her in his bedroom as well as his kitchen.

Her gran's severe bout of bronchitis during the winter two years ago had given Poppy the perfect excuse to move back home and follow her dream. Setting up the tearoom had been a way of bringing in a modest income whilst being able to keep an eye on her gran, and not for a day had she regretted doing it.

Poppy blew out a breath as she made her way inside the house. Maybe she did have a bias against successful men, as Raffaele Caffarelli had suggested. But why shouldn't she resent him for thinking he could buy whatever or whoever he took a fancy to? He might be incredibly good-looking, with bucket loads of charm, but she was *not* going to be his next conquest.

She would stake money on it. Well, she would if she had any, of course.

Rafe strode into his London office on Monday morning. 'Did you get that information for me?'

Margaret handed him a folder. 'There's not much, but what I've got is in there. So, how was your weekend?'

'Average.' He started flicking through the papers as he walked through to his office. 'Hold my calls, will you?'

'What if Miss Silverton calls?'

Rafe thought about it for a beat. 'Make her wait.'

Margaret's brows lifted. 'Will do.'

He closed his office door and took the folder over to his desk. There wasn't much he didn't already know. Poppy Silverton had grown up with her grandmother in the dower house on the Dalrymple Estate and had been educated locally before moving to London in her late teens. She had trained as a chef and had worked in a restaurant in Soho he'd been to a couple of times. She'd been running the tearoom in the village for the last couple of years. Her grandmother, Beatrice, had died a few months ago, exactly six months after Lord Dalrymple, and the house he had left to Beatrice had subsequently passed to Poppy.

Rafe leaned back in his chair. There was nothing about her private life, about who she was dating or had dated. He couldn't help a rueful smile. If a similar search had been done on him or one of his brothers, reams and reams of stuff would have come spilling out.

He'd driven away from the manor late on Saturday night but he hadn't stopped thinking about her. It wasn't just her house that was playing on his mind. He'd never met a more intriguing woman. She was so spirited and defiant. She must realise she hadn't a hope of winning against him, but she stood up to him all the same. That was enormously attractive. He was so used to women tripping over themselves to please him.

But Poppy's comment about him not knowing who genuinely cared for him had resonated a little too well with him. Apart from his brothers, who really gave a toss about him? His grandfather certainly didn't. His members of staff were respectful and mostly loyal, but then he paid them generously to be so.

He frowned at where his thoughts were heading. He wasn't interested in love and commitment. Losing his parents had taught him to keep a very tight lid on his emotions. Loving someone hurt like hell if you lost them. He never lost anything or anyone now. He did the hiring and the firing in all of his relationships.

They lasted as long as he wanted and no longer.

Rafe leaned forward to press the intercom on his desk. 'Margaret? Find out who owns the building Miss Silverton operates her tearoom out of. Make them an offer they can't refuse. Get them to sign a confidentiality agreement.'

'Right away.'

'Oh, and one other thing… Cancel all of my appointments for the next couple of weeks. I'm heading out of town.'

'A holiday?'

Rafe smiled to himself. 'You could call it that.'

CHAPTER THREE

POPPY WAS WAITING on one of her regulars when Raffaele Caffarelli came in the following Monday. She tried to ignore the little skip of her pulse and focused her attention on Mr Compton who came in at the same time every day and had done so ever since his wife of sixty-six years had died. 'There you are, Mr Compton,' she said as she handed the elderly gentleman a generous slice of his favourite orange-and-coconut cake.

'Thank you, my dear,' Mr Compton said. 'Where's your offsider today?'

'She's visiting her mother,' Poppy said, conscious of Raffaele's black-as-night gaze on her. 'Can I get you a fresh pot of tea? More cream for your cake? Another slice to take home for your supper?'

'No, love, you'd better serve your other customer.' Mr Compton gave her a wink. 'Things are finally looking up, eh?'

Poppy gave him a forced smile as she mentally rolled her eyes. 'I wish.' She went to where Raffaele was standing. 'A table for one?'

His dark eyes glinted. 'Thank you.'

She led him to a table near the window. 'A double-shot espresso, no sugar?'

His mouth twitched at the corners. 'You have a good memory.'

Poppy tried not to look at his mouth. It was *so* distracting. So too were his hands. She could still feel the imprint of those long, tanned fingers around her wrist. She felt shivery every time she recalled them against her white skin. His touch had been unforgettable. Her body still hummed with the memory of it.

He was dressed casually in blue denim jeans and an open-necked white shirt with the sleeves rolled up past his strong, tanned wrists. He had twelve to eighteen hours of stubble on his jaw. He smelt divine—a hint of wood and citrus and healthy, potent, virile male. He oozed with sex appeal. She felt the invisible current of it pass over her skin. It made her heart pick up its pace as if he had reached out and touched her.

Poppy put her chin up to a pert level. ‘I don’t suppose I can tempt you with a slice of cake?’

His eyes smouldered as they held hers. ‘I’m very tempted.’

She pursed her lips and spoke in an undertone in case Mr Compton overheard, which was highly unlikely, given he was as deaf as the proverbial post, but still. ‘*Cake*, Mr Caffarelli. I’m offering you cake.’

‘Just the coffee.’ He waited a beat. ‘For now.’

Poppy swung away to the kitchen, furious with him, but even more furious with herself for being so affected by him. She’d been expecting him to come back. She had tried not to watch out for him but every morning she had looked towards the manor to see if his flashy sports car was parked out front. She had tried her best to ignore the little dip of disappointment in the pit of her belly when it had failed to appear. She knew he wasn’t going to give up on trying to acquire the dower house any time soon.

She had read up on him in some gossip magazines Chloe had given her. He had a reputation for being ruthless in business. 'Single-minded, stealthy and steely in terms of determination', one reporter had said.

Poppy suspected he was equally ruthless in his sensual conquests. His latest mistress was a bikini model with a figure to die for. Poppy couldn't imagine a slice of cake or a chocolate-chip cookie ever passing through those filler-enhanced lips.

She carried the coffee out to him. 'Will there be anything else?'

'What time do you close?'

'Five or thereabouts,' she said. 'I try to be flexible in case I get late-comers. No one likes being rushed over their cup of tea.' She gave his cup a pointed look before adding, 'Or coffee.'

His coal-black gaze glinted again. 'I have some business I'd like to discuss with you.'

Poppy stiffened. 'I'm not selling my house.'

'It's nothing to do with the dower house.'

She looked at him guardedly. 'So…what is it about?'

'I'm spending a couple of weeks at the manor

to get a feel for the place before I start drawing up plans for the development,' he said. 'I don't want to employ a housekeeper at this stage. Are you interested in providing dinner each day? I'll pay you handsomely, of course.'

Poppy chewed at her lower lip for a moment. She could do with the money, but cooking him dinner each night? What else would he expect from her—her body dished up as a dessert? 'What's wrong with eating at the village pub? They do a pretty good bar snack. *There was no way she was going to recommend he try Oliver's restaurant.*

He gave her a droll look. 'I don't eat bar snacks.'

She gave her eyes a little roll. 'Of course you don't.'

'Blame my mother. She was French. You know what the French are like with their food.'

Mr Compton shuffled over on his walking frame. 'Do it, Poppy. It'll be a nice little earner for you to tide you over this rough patch.'

Poppy wished she hadn't let slip to Mr Compton a couple of weeks ago how tight things were. She didn't want Raffaele Caffarelli gaining any sort of advantage over her. He was ruthless and calculating. How far would he go to get what he wanted? 'Can I think about it and get back to you?' she said.

Rafe handed her a business card. 'Call me tonight.'

She put the card in her apron pocket and turned to speak to her only other customer. 'I'll just get that slice of cake for you to take home, Mr Compton.'

Rafe held out his hand to the elderly gentleman once Poppy had disappeared into the kitchen. 'Rafe Caffarelli,' he said.

'Howard Compton.' The old man shook his hand. 'So, you're the new owner of Dalrymple Manor.'

'Yes. I've had my eye on it for a while. It's a great piece of real estate.'

'It is at that,' Mr Compton said. 'What do you plan to do with it?'

'I'm turning it into a luxury hotel and spa.'

'Don't go telling Poppy that.' Mr Compton gave him a twinkling smile. 'She wanted a family to buy the place. It's a long time since one lived there, mind you.'

'Were you acquainted with Lord Dalrymple?'

'His wife and mine were best friends since childhood,' Mr Compton said. 'It was a terrible day when Clara died. Henry became reclusive after that. If it weren't for Poppy's grandmother Beatrice he would have curled up and died. We thought it was a nice gesture of his to leave the dower house to her and Poppy. A lot of the locals thought he would leave the whole estate to them, but there would've been too much of an outcry from the extended family if he'd done that. As it was probate took over a year to come through. So messy when there isn't a direct heir.'

Rafe thought about his own situation. He had no direct heirs other than his brothers. Who would inherit his vast fortune? He hadn't really thought about it until now… Why was he working so hard if he had no one to leave it to?

He pushed the thought aside. There was plenty of time to think about marriage. He was only thirty-five. It wasn't like he had a biological clock to worry about. Some time in the future he would select a suitable woman, someone who knew how to move in the circles he moved in, someone who wouldn't encroach on his freedom too much.

Poppy came back carrying a foil-wrapped parcel. 'Here you go, Mr Compton.'

'You're a pet,' Mr Compton said. 'I don't know what I'd do without you.' He turned back to Rafe. 'Nice to meet you, Rafe. Drop by some time and have a wee dram with me. I'm at Bramble Cottage in Briar Lane. You can't miss it.'

'I'd like that very much,' Rafe said and was almost surprised that he meant it. He gave himself a mental shake. What was he thinking? He wasn't here to make friends. He was here to make money.

The bell over the door tinkled as the old man left.

'I can see your charm isn't exclusively aimed at the female of the species,' Poppy said, casting him a cynical look.

'He's a lovely old man,' Rafe said. 'And quite lonely, I suspect.'

'He is…' Her shoulders went down on a little sigh as she sank her teeth into her lower lip for a beat. 'I do what I can for him but I can't bring back his wife. They were best friends. It's so sad. I guess that's the downside of finding the love of your life. Eventually you have to lose them.'

'Isn't it supposedly better to have loved and lost than never to have loved at all?'

She turned away and began clearing Mr Compton's cup and saucer and plate with brisk officiousness. 'What about your latest girlfriend? Is she coming to stay with you at the manor?'

'I'm currently unattached.'

She glanced back at him over her shoulder with a raised eyebrow. 'Your choice or hers?'

'Mine.' It was *always* his choice. He wouldn't have it any other way.

'She was very beautiful.'

'Until she opened her mouth.'

She gave him an arch look. 'Couldn't you think of other ways to keep her mouth occupied?'

Right now Rafe could only think of Poppy's mouth, how it was so rosy and plump and totally natural. His groin began to thrum with desire as he thought of her velvet lips around him, her soft little tongue licking or stroking him. He wanted to taste her mouth, to sample the texture of her lips, to taste the sweetness of her, to stroke into the warm moistness of her.

What was it about her that was so damn alluring? She wasn't his type at all with her feisty little looks and combative poses. Most of the time she looked like she wanted to scratch his eyes out, but now and again he would catch a glimpse of something else in her gaze, something much more exciting—earthy, primal lust. She tried to hide it but he could sense it in her body: the way she carried herself, holding herself stiffly as if she was frightened her body would suddenly do something out of her control.

Her buttoned-up sensuality was intoxicatingly attractive. He suspected she would be dynamite once she let herself go. Her touch had electrified him the other day. He still felt the buzz of where her fingers had brushed him. He wanted those dainty little fingers all over his body. He wanted to be *inside* her body. He was rock-hard just thinking about how she would feel wrapped tightly around him. It would be a conflagration of the senses, a combustible explosion of fire meeting ice. 'What about you, Miss Silverton?'

Her expression became guarded. 'What about me?'

'Are you currently involved with anyone?'

Her gaze narrowed. 'I find it hard to see why it could be of any interest to you if I am or if I'm not.'

'*Au contraire*,' he said. 'I find it immensely interesting.'

Her cheeks flared with colour but her eyes were glittering with spirited defiance. 'Would you like more coffee, Mr Caffarelli, or shall I get your bill?'

Rafe held that sparkling toffee-brown gaze and felt his blood heat up another notch. He could smell her light fragrance. He was close enough to touch her. He felt the tension in her body; it was pulsing just below the surface. She was doing everything she could to hide it but he was aware of it all the same. Hate and lust were swirling in the air like a powerful, heady aroma. 'You don't like me very much, do you?'

Her mouth tightened primly. 'My job is to serve you coffee, not become your best friend.'

He gave her a lazy half-smile. 'Haven't you heard that saying, "keep your friends close, but your enemies closer"?'

Her eyes flashed at him as she pointedly handed him the bill for his coffee. 'Haven't you heard the saying, "there's no such thing as a free lunch"?'

Rafe chuckled as he took out his wallet, peeled off a tenner and placed it on the table beside her. 'Until we meet again, Miss Silverton. *Ciao*.'

Poppy was about to go to bed when she noticed Chutney was missing. The three dogs had been out in the garden while she had a bath, but when she called them back in only Pickles and Relish appeared. 'Chutney?' she called out from the back door. 'Chutney? Here boy. Come and get a treat.'

There was no sign of him in the garden. He seemed to have completely vanished. It was hard not to worry after what had happened to Pickles. Poppy had found him injured after finding a gap in the hedge leading to the field in front of Dalrymple Manor. It had been so harrowing to find him lying in the long grass, whimpering in pain.

Her heart began to stammer. Chutney had a tendency to wander, especially if he got the scent of a rabbit. Even though she had got the gap in the hedge fixed, she suspected there were other places he could have squeezed through, being so much smaller than the other two dogs. What if he had got out on the road? Although there wasn't much traffic along this particular lane, it only took one speeding car to do the damage.

Poppy looked at the manor in the distance. Raffaele Caffarelli's top-notch sports car was parked out the front. There were lights on downstairs, which meant he must be still awake.

She glanced at the business card on the kitchen table. Should she call him to see if he had seen any sign of Chutney? The three dogs were used to walking up to the manor. Before Lord Dalrymple had died she had taken them up every day to visit, and she had only stopped walking them in the grounds of the manor once the 'sold' sign had gone up.

She picked up the business card and ran her

index finger over his name. She took a little uneven breath, reached for her phone and quickly typed in the number before she changed her mind. He answered on the third ring.

'Rafe Caffarelli.'

Poppy felt the base of her spine shiver at the sound of the deep burr of his voice. 'Um…it's Poppy Silverton here.'

'I've been expecting you to call.'

'I'm not calling about the dinner thing. I wondered if you'd seen a little dog up at the manor.'

'What sort of dog?'

'He's a cavoodle.'

'A what?'

Poppy rolled her eyes at his tone. 'He's a cross between a miniature poodle and a King Charles cavalier. He's called Chutney.'

'You named your dog after a condiment?'

She pursed her mouth in irritation. 'Have you seen him or not?'

'No.'

'Fine,' she said. 'I'm sorry to bother you so late. Goodni—'

'I'll have a look around outside. Would he have

wandered into the maze, do you think? I haven't figured it out yet so you might have to come and rescue me from the minotaur if I get stuck.'

'I'm sure you're quite adept at getting yourself out of complicated situations.'

He gave a little chuckle. 'You've been reading up on me, haven't you?'

'If you find Chutney, please call me.'

'I'll do even better than that. I'll deliver him to your door.'

'I wouldn't want to put you to any bother.'

'Will he come to a stranger?'

'He's a shameless glutton,' Poppy said. 'He'll do anything for food.'

Her spine shivered again as he gave another deep chuckle. 'I know the type.'

The doorbell rang a few minutes later. Poppy had only just come back inside after doing another round of the garden. She shushed Pickles and Relish, who were bouncing up and down on their back legs like string puppets being controlled by a hyperactive puppeteer. 'Down, Pickles; you too, Relish. Sit. I said *sit*.' She opened the door to find Rafe standing there with Chutney under one arm. 'Oh, you found him! Where was he?'

He handed the dog to her. 'He was sitting at the back of the manor near the kitchen door.'

Poppy put Chutney on the floor where his two friends immediately besieged him with frenzied licks and whimpers of delight, as if he'd been away for a month instead of an hour. She straightened to face Rafe. 'I'm sorry about that. I think he still misses Lord Dalrymple. We used to go up to visit him every day.'

'I noticed he seemed quite at home.'

'Yes, well, I made a habit of wandering past with the dogs to check the place wasn't vandalised while it was vacant,' Poppy said. 'I'm not going up there now, of course.'

His eyes glinted knowingly. 'Of course.'

She straightened her shoulders. 'Thank you for returning him. You didn't have to. I would have come to collect him. All you had to do was call me.'

'Have you thought about my dinner proposal?'

Poppy felt that funny little shiver again as his dark eyes held hers. She wasn't exactly dressed for visitors. She was wearing the oldest, shabbiest tracksuit she possessed and a pair of scruffy old trainers that had holes over her big toes where Pickles had chewed them. Her hair was tied up with a ribbon and her face bare of make-up. It made her feel at a distinct disadvantage. It made her feel about ten years old. Why, oh why hadn't she changed into something a little less unsophisticated? 'Um, I think you should ask someone else,' she said.

'I want you.'

Heat flowed into her cheeks as that coal-black gaze smouldered against hers. 'I'm not available.' To her chagrin her voice sounded throaty and husky...*sexy, even.*

'You know you want to say yes. I can see it in your eyes.'

Poppy glowered at him. 'I can see why you fly everywhere by private jet—you'd need all the extra cabin space for your ego.'

A smile lurked around the corners of his mouth. 'You're a stubborn little thing, aren't you?'

'I did warn you.'

'Likewise.' His black-as-pitch gaze held hers

with a glint of implacable determination. 'When I want something, I don't give up until I have it.'

'Thank you for bringing Chutney home,' she said holding the door open for him. 'Don't let me keep you.'

Those dark-as-night eyes lowered to her mouth for a moment before returning to mesh with her gaze. 'Aren't you going to do the neighbourly thing and invite me in for a night-cap since I so gallantly returned your dog?'

Poppy knew it would appear churlish of her to refuse him entry. But wouldn't inviting him in so late at night send him the message she actually *wanted* his company?

Of course she didn't want his company. She had plenty of company. She had her three little dogs, didn't she? 'I'm kind of busy right now.'

'I'm house-trained, if that's what's worrying you.' His hint of a smile was devastatingly attractive. 'I won't cock my leg on the furniture or try and bury bones in the backyard.'

'I'm not in the habit of inviting men I barely know into my house late at night.'

Was that a glimmer of respect she saw in his

eyes? 'Are you worried about what the neighbours will think?' he asked.

'You're the only neighbour for miles,' she pointed out.

A more serious note entered his voice and was reflected in his gaze as it held hers. 'You're quite safe with me, Miss Silverton. I might have a reputation but I have the utmost respect for women and always have.'

'How reassuring.'

'You don't believe me.'

'Some of the comments your ex-mistress posted online about you were rather derogatory,' Poppy said.

'It's not my best character reference, that's for sure. But she was unhappy about being made redundant, so to speak. I'll get my secretary to send her a parting gift to soften the blow. It was remiss of me not to think of it earlier. I bet once Zandra gets several thousand pounds' worth of rubies or sapphires she'll take the comments down.'

Poppy arched her brow at him. 'Why not diamonds?'

'I never give diamonds.'

'Why not? It's not as if you can't afford them.'

'Diamonds are for ever,' he said. 'When I find the right girl to give them to, I'll buy them, but not before.'

Poppy gave him a sceptical look. 'So you're actually planning to give up your partying and playboy lifestyle at some point?'

His shrug was noncommittal. 'It's not on my immediate agenda.'

She couldn't keep the derision from her tone or from the angle of her chin. 'Too busy out there sowing your wild oats?'

His eyes glinted as they held hers. 'There are a few fresh fields I have yet to plough. After that, who knows? Don't they say reformed rakes make the best husbands?'

'What sort of wife will you require?' Poppy asked. 'A plaster saint with a blue-blooded background similar to your own?'

A sparkle of playfulness entered his gaze. 'Are you thinking of auditioning for the post?'

She pulled her chin back in against her throat. 'You must be joking. You're the very last person I would ever think of marrying.'

He gave her a mock bow before he turned to leave. 'The feeling is mutual, Miss Silverton. *Bonsoir.*'

CHAPTER FOUR

'I JUST RAN into Mr Compton on my way to work,' Chloe said the following morning. 'He said Rafe Caffarelli came in again yesterday.'

'He just had coffee.' Poppy turned to put the cream she had just whipped back in the fridge. 'Quite frankly, I don't know why he bothers. What's the point of going to a tearoom if you don't drink tea and you don't eat cake?'

'Mr Compton also told me Rafe asked you to provide evening meals for him up at the manor.' Chloe picked up her apron and began to tie it around her waist. 'That's exciting. The way to a man's heart and all that. What are you going to cook for him?'

'I'm not cooking for him.'

Chloe blinked. 'Are you crazy? He's going to pay you, isn't he?'

Poppy set her mouth stubbornly. 'That's not the point.'

'*I'll* cook for him, then,' Chloe said. 'I'll do three meals a day and morning and afternoon tea. I'll even give him breakfast in bed. God, I'm having a hot flush just thinking about it. I bet he's amazing between the sheets. He looks like he pumps some serious iron. I bet he could go all night.'

Poppy gave her a withering look. 'There is more to a man than how he looks. What about intellect and morals? What about personal values?'

Chloe grinned at her. 'You fancy him like rotten, don't you? Go on—admit it. And I reckon he fancies you. Mr Compton reckons so too. Why else would he come in for coffee two days in a row?'

Poppy stalked over to put the cupcakes on the glass cake-stand. 'Raffaele Caffarelli has had more lovers than you and I have had hot dinners. He thinks that just because he wants something or someone he can have it. His sense of entitlement is beyond arrogant. It's deplorable.'

Chloe's eyes began to twinkle. 'You really are all fired up over him, aren't you? This can't just be about your house. Why do you dislike him so much?'

Poppy carried the cake-stand out to the tea-room. 'I'd rather not talk about it.'

Chloe followed close behind. 'Mr Compton said Rafe's going to turn Dalrymple Manor into a luxury hotel and spa. It could be really good for the village if he does. There'd be heaps of jobs for the locals, and we might even get a bit of extra business as a result.'

Poppy plonked the cake-stand down and turned to glare her. 'For the last four-hundred-and-seventy-five years, the manor has been a family home. Generations of the Dalrymple family have been born and have died there. Turning it into a plush hotel will totally destroy its character and desecrate its history.'

'I expect Rafe Caffarelli will do a very tasteful conversion,' Chloe put in. 'I checked out some of his other developments online. He's big on keeping things in context architecturally. He draws up most of the preliminary plans himself.'

Poppy was still on her soapbox and wasn't stepping down any time soon. The thought of the paparazzi hiding in the hedges in her beloved village to get their prized shot of hedonistic celebrities partying up at the manor was sickening. 'Lord Dalrymple will be spinning in his grave if this preposterous project goes ahead. What was his cousin thinking of, selling to a developer? Why couldn't they have sold to a private family instead? Another family could bring life and vibrancy to the place instead of filthy rich people wining and dining and partying at all hours.'

'You really love that old place, don't you?'

Poppy blew out a long breath. 'I know it sounds ridiculously sentimental but I think Dalrymple Manor needs a family to make it come alive again. It's spent the last sixty years grieving. You can feel the sadness when you walk in there. It's almost palpable. The stairs creak with it, sometimes even the foundations groan with it.'

Chloe's eyes rounded. 'Are you saying it's haunted?'

'I used to think so when I was a kid, but no, it's

just a sad old place that needs to be filled with love and laughter and family again.'

'Maybe Rafe Caffarelli will settle down there with one of his lovers,' Chloe suggested.

'I can't see that happening,' Poppy said with an expression of disdain. 'He doesn't keep a lover more than a month or two. Playboys like him don't settle down, they just change partners.'

Chloe gave her a speculative look. 'So I take it I'm not the only one who's done a little online searching on the illustrious Rafe Caffarelli?'

Poppy went back to the kitchen with her head at a haughty height. 'I'm not the least bit interested in what that man does or who he does it with. I have much better things to do with my time.'

Just before lunch Mr Underwood, Poppy's landlord, came in to the tearoom. He usually came in on a Friday afternoon for a cup of tea and a slice of the cake of the day. Poppy desperately hoped this Tuesday visit wasn't a business one. She had a list of expenses to see to on the dower house. The place needed painting inside and out, and the garden needed urgent attention. There was an elm tree close to her bedroom that needed lopping as it was keeping her awake at night with its branches scratching at the window. Even a modest rise in rent at the shop would just about cripple her financially now.

'Your usual, Mr Underwood?' she said with a bright and hopeful smile.

'Er, can I have a word, Poppy?' John Underwood asked.

'Sure.' Poppy's smile tightened on her face. *Please don't ask for more rent.*

'I thought I should let you know I've been made an offer on the building,' John said. 'It's a good one, the best I've had, so I'm going to take it.'

She frowned. 'But I didn't realise you were even thinking of selling.'

'I've been toying with the idea for a while. Jean wants to travel a bit more. We've got three young grandchildren in the States now and we want to spend a bit more time with them. I'm selling this building and another investment property I have in Shropshire.'

Poppy felt suspicion move up her spine like a file of sugar ants. 'Who made the offer?'

'I'm not at liberty to say,' he said. 'The buyer insisted on total confidentiality until all the paperwork is done.'

She pursed her lips as the rage simmered inside her. 'I just bet he did.'

John looked uncomfortable. 'I didn't want to do the wrong thing by you, Poppy. You and Chloe are the best tenants I've had. But at the end of the day this is a business decision. It's not personal.'

Oh yes it is, Poppy thought sourly. 'We've still got another year on the lease. That won't change, will it?'

'Not unless the new owner wants to redevelop.'

'Did he say what he intended to do with it?'

'No, he just seemed really keen to acquire this particular building. He said he instantly fell in love with its old-world charm.'

'Ruthless' didn't even come close to describing Rafe Caffarelli, Poppy thought. He was clever and calculating, much more than she had realised. But she wasn't going down without a fight. There was no way she was going to let him have things all his own way. Did he really think he could twist her arm? Blackmail her into his bed by charging her an outrageously high rent? What sort of woman did he think she was? 'Will the new owner expect a rise in rent, do you think?'

'You'd have to discuss that with him.'

She gave him an ironic look. 'How can I if he wants to remain anonymous?'

'I expect the rent will be handled through an agency,' John said. 'Anyway, I just thought I should let you know I've sold. I'm not one for keeping secrets but he seemed to think it was necessary.'

Poppy ground her teeth behind her tight smile. 'I'm sure he has his reasons.'

She stalked out to the kitchen once John Underwood had left. 'Grrrh! I'm going to punch him on the nose. I'm going to scratch his eyes out. I'm going to give him a black eye. I'm going to kick him in the you-know-where.'

Chloe blinked in confusion. 'But I thought you liked Mr Underwood. What's he done—put up the rent or something?'

'Not Mr Underwood,' Poppy said through clenched teeth. 'Rafe Caffarelli. He's bought the shop. I know it's him, even though Mr Underwood didn't actually say so. It's supposed to be a secret. And I know why—Rafe Caffarelli wants to blackmail me into his bed.'

Chloe's eyes nearly popped out of her head. 'Hey, have I missed something somewhere? Back up a little bit. Did you say he wants to *sleep* with you? Did he actually say that out loud?'

'Not in as many words, but I can see it in his eyes every time he looks at me.' Poppy clenched her hands into fists. 'I *won't* do it.'

'*I'll* do it,' Chloe said. 'What are you thinking, Poppy? He's gorgeous. He's rich. He's everything a woman could want in a man.'

Poppy set her mouth. 'Not *this* woman.'

'You're mad,' Chloe said. 'What would it hurt to have a little fling with him? He would probably give you heaps and heaps of ridiculously expensive jewellery at the end of it. You could sell them and retire.'

Poppy threw her a look of reproach. 'I had no idea you were so shallow.'

Chloe shrugged. 'Not shallow, just pragmatic. Think about it. When are you going to get the chance to move in his sort of circles? It'd be worth it just for the publicity. It'd really put the tearoom on the map.'

'I am *not* going to sleep with Rafe Caffarelli in order to bring more customers in the door.' Poppy folded her arms tightly across her chest. 'I have far more self-respect than that.'

'You're stuck in the dark ages,' Chloe said. 'Who waits for Mr Right these days? Most girls lose their virginity before they leave school. You're twenty-five for God's sake. Think of all the sex you're going to have to have to catch up.'

'I don't think about sex.' *Well, not until recently.*

'That's because you don't know what you're missing. It's not wrong to have sex before you get married. Not in this day and age.'

'I'm not necessarily waiting until I get married,' Poppy said. 'I'm waiting until I feel sure it's really what I want, and that the man is right for me.'

'It's because of what happened to your mum, isn't it?' Chloe said. 'It's made you gun-shy.'

'Maybe a bit,' Poppy confessed. 'OK, more than a bit. It ruined her life to be cast aside like that. She *never* got over it. She was truly heart-broken. She loved my father and he treated her like a silly little toy he had grown tired of. And it didn't just wreck her life, it ruined my gran's life because she got landed with a little kid to bring up.'

'Your gran loved bringing you up.'

Poppy let out a sigh. 'But my mother died so young and she didn't get to do all the things she wanted to do. I don't want that to happen to me. I want to have control over my future.'

'There are some things in life that you just can't control.'

'I know, but I'm going to focus on the ones I can.' Poppy untied her apron and tossed it on the nearest chair. 'Starting right now.'

Rafe was working on some preliminary sketches in the makeshift study he'd set up at the manor when he heard a car rumble up the driveway. He knew who it was without looking through the window. Only someone with an axe to grind would slam their car door, stomp across the gravel, to put their finger on the doorbell and leave it there. He smiled as the tinny sound assaulted his eardrums. How boring had his life been before meeting Poppy Silverton?

This was the most fun he'd had in years.

'We have to stop meeting like this,' he said as he opened the door. 'People will talk.'

Her toffee-brown eyes were slitted, her hands were fisted and her slim body was rigid. 'You… you calculating, low-life swine.'

He raised a brow at her. 'It's nice to see you too.'

She vibrated on the spot like a battery-operated tin soldier. 'I can't believe how ruthless you are. You bought my shop!'

'So? I'm a property developer. I buy property.'

Her pretty little mouth was white-tipped with fury. 'I know what you're doing but it won't work.'

Rafe leaned casually against the doorjamb. 'What is it you think I'm doing?'

'You're going to blackmail me.' She glowered at him darkly. 'You must know I can barely afford the rent as it is. But it won't work. I won't prostitute myself to someone like you.'

He tapped his index finger against his lips for a moment. 'Mmm, I can see I have some work to do to improve the impression you have of me. What makes you think I'm going to raise the rent?'

She looked at him warily. 'You mean...you're not?'

He shook his head.

'But why did you buy the shop?'

'I like it.'

She narrowed her eyes again. 'You...*like* it?'

'It's unique.'

'What do you mean?'

'I like the idea of a traditional tearoom. It's classy. It makes a nice change from the somewhat impersonal and boring coffee chains.'

A little pleat of scepticism appeared between her eyes. 'You don't even drink tea.'

'That's true, but maybe I haven't tasted the perfect cup. A cheap, dusty tea bag jiggled in a Styrofoam cup is probably nothing like the real deal. Maybe you could educate me in the art of drinking proper, high-quality leaf tea.'

She was still looking at him in suspicion.

'Why do I get the feeling you're not really talking about tea?'

Rafe gave her a lazy smile. 'What else could I be talking about?'

Her cheeks went a deep shade of rose and her soft mouth flattened primly. 'If you want to taste proper tea, then come to the tearoom four o'clock this afternoon.'

He held her gaze in a smouldering little lockdown. 'I'd prefer a private lesson. I don't want to be distracted by other customers. It might ruin the experience for me.'

She gave him a flinty 'I know what you're up to' look. 'All right,' she said. 'Come at five-thirty. I'll put the closed sign on the door.'

'It's a date.'

Rafe watched as she turned on her heel and stomped back to her car. He gave her a wave as she drove away but she didn't return it. With a toss of that fiery head, she put her car into gear and rattled off down the drive, leaving a billowing cloud of dust in her wake.

CHAPTER FIVE

CHLOE UNTIED HER apron at five o'clock. 'I just got a call from my mum. She wants me to pick up some of her asthma medication at the pharmacy on my way home. Do you mind if I leave now?'

Poppy tried to ignore the little flutter of alarm in her belly. She didn't mind giving Rafe Caffarelli a private lesson in the art of tea drinking, but she hadn't planned on it being *that* private. She had banked on Chloe being in the background in case he wanted to have his cake and eat it too, so to speak. 'No, you go,' she said, releasing a little breath of resignation. 'Say hi to your mum from me. Take her some of that double-chocolate slice she likes so much.'

Chloe's smile was teasing. 'Will you be all right entertaining the deliciously ruthless, rich and racy Rafe Caffarelli on your little ownsome?'

Poppy put on a confident smile that in no way reflected how she was feeling. 'Of course.'

The door chime sounded at five-thirty-five. Poppy had been watching the clock ever since Chloe had left. As each minute had crawled by, her heart rate had gone up. She came out of the kitchen as casually as she could even though her stomach was pitching and falling like a paper-boat in a jacuzzi.

Rafe stooped as he came in the door. He was dressed a little more formally this time in charcoal-grey trousers and a crisp white shirt teamed with a dark-blue blazer and a silver-grey tie. He had shaved since she had seen him earlier that day. He had showered too, as his hair was still damp and had the groove marks in it from a brush or comb.

'I'm sorry I'm late.'

Poppy couldn't read his expression, but she knew one thing for certain—he wasn't one bit sorry. 'I've set up the table by the window. Take a seat while I put the kettle on.'

'Can't I watch?'

She pursed her lips at him. His dark eyes were

pools of black ink but there was a hint of amusement lurking there; she was sure of it. 'I can assure you there's nothing remotely interesting in watching a kettle come to the boil.'

'There is if you're the one boiling it.'

She gave him a schoolmarmish look. 'Are you flirting with me, Mr Caffarelli?'

'Call me Rafe.'

'Rafe…' Poppy felt like she had crossed an invisible line by calling him by his preferred name.

His eyes held hers in an intimate tether. It felt like another line had been crossed, a far more intimate one. Her gaze went to his mouth, as if pulled there by a powerful magnet. Her lips tingled as she wondered what it would feel like to have his pressed against them. Would he kiss firmly or with seductive softness? She felt a tiny shiver pass over her skin as her thoughts continued on their erotic journey… What would it feel like to have his hands cup her breasts or stroke between her…?

'Poppy.'

'Yes?' Her tongue made a quick darting movement over her lips.

His mouth tilted in a sexy smile. 'It's a cute name. It suits you.'

Cute? He didn't think she was stunningly beautiful or gorgeous, just cute, like a puppy or a kitten. 'Thank you.' She gave him a tight, on-off smile. 'Um…the kitchen's this way.'

Poppy went through the motion of putting on the kettle but the whole time she was aware of Rafe's impossibly dark gaze resting on her. She told him how it was important to fill the kettle with fresh cold water each time, and how it was important to warm the teapot before spooning in the leaves—one for each person and one for the pot. 'Tea always tastes nicer from a china cup,' she said. 'Cheap thick, chunky mugs just don't cut it, I'm afraid.'

He was looking at her with a smile lurking in those coal-black eyes. 'Fascinating.'

'Yes, well, I admit I'm a bit old-school about it, but there you go.' She put a hand-knitted cosy on the teapot and placed it on the tray she had laid out earlier.

'Let me carry that for you.'

She felt the brush of his fingers against hers as

he took the tray. It felt like a charge of electricity shooting to that secret place between her thighs.

Her eyes locked with his for a pulsing moment. His eyes were so dark she couldn't see where his pupils began or ended. She could smell the clean, male scent of him—the subtle hint of lemon and lime with an understory of something woody and fresh, like a native pine forest. This close she could see the individual pinpoints of his cleanly shaven jaw. Within a few hours it would be dark and prickly around that sculptured mouth and determined chin. Even now it would rasp if she touched it with the softness of her fingertips…

Poppy curled her fingertips into her palm and shifted her gaze away from his. 'Right… Well, let's go and have tea.'

Once the table was set up, Rafe guided her to her seat with a hand at her elbow. Poppy felt another shiver shimmy up her spine at the contact of his skin on hers. She couldn't recall a time when she had been more acutely aware of a man. Everything about him stirred her senses until she could hardly get her brain to focus on the task at hand.

'Um…do you take milk?'

'I don't know.' He gave her a wry smile. 'Should I?'

'It rather depends on the type of tea,' Poppy said. 'I drink English breakfast with milk, but I drink Earl Grey, Darjeeling, Russian Caravan and Jasmine black. But at the end of the day, it's all a matter of personal taste.'

'Give it to me straight, just like my coffee.'

She poured him a cup and watched as he took a taste. He wrinkled up his nose and put the cup back down in its saucer.

'Well?'

'It's a bit flavourless.'

'*Flavourless?*'

'Bland.'

'It's the highest quality Ceylon tea, for God's sake,' Poppy said. 'What is *wrong* with your taste buds?'

'Nothing's wrong with my taste buds. I just don't like tea.'

'How about if you try it with some milk and sugar?'

'I'll try the milk but not the sugar.' He gave her a heart-stopping smile. 'I'm sweet enough.'

Poppy rolled her eyes. 'Here.' She handed him his cup again. 'Taste it now.'

He went through the same routine, wrinkling up his nose as he took a tentative sip. He put the cup back down again. 'Doesn't float my boat, I'm afraid.'

'You don't like it?'

'It's nondescript.'

'It's not nondescript,' she said. 'It's subtle.'

'It's just not my cup of tea.' He flashed her that grin again. 'Sorry, no pun intended.'

Poppy shook her head at him, trying not to smile. He could be incredibly charming when he put his mind to it. She would have to be careful not to let her guard down. He was the enemy. It wouldn't do to think of him as anything else. 'You're incorrigible.'

'That's what my mother used to say.'

There was something almost wistful about his tone. She wondered if he was close to his family. She picked up her own cup and took a sip. 'Where do your parents live? In France or Italy?'

The light had gone out of his eyes. 'They don't.'

'Pardon?'

'They don't live anywhere. They're dead. They were killed when I was ten.'

'I'm sorry…' Poppy bit her lip. Maybe she should have done a little more research on him. The article she had come across had mentioned nothing about his childhood, only about his playboy status, wealth and the latest lover he'd been with.

'It was a long time ago.'

'What happened?'

He picked up his teaspoon and began toying with it between his finger and thumb like one would do a pen. 'They had a high-speed collision with another motorboat on the French Rivera. My mother was killed instantly. My father died in hospital three days later from internal injuries.'

'I'm so sorry… It must have been a terrible time for you and your brothers.'

A flicker of pain passed through his eyes before he lowered them to look at the spoon he was holding. 'Yes. It was.'

'What happened afterwards? I mean…where did you go? Who looked after you and your brothers?'

'My paternal grandfather took us in.' He put down the spoon, picked up his teacup and cradled it in his hands.

'Is he still alive?'

'Yes.'

'Are you close to him?'

His lip curled but not in a smile. 'No one is close to my grandfather.'

Poppy could tell he wasn't keen to reveal too much about his background. But his cryptic comment about his grandfather was rather intriguing. What sort of man was Vittorio Caffarelli? Had he made the lives of the three bereaved boys even more miserable in his handling and rearing of them? 'What about your grandmother? Was she involved in your upbringing?'

'No, she died of cancer when my father was a teenager.'

'What about your maternal grandparents?'

Rafe turned the cup around in its saucer. 'They died before I was born.' He picked up the cup and took a sip, grimacing at the taste before he put it back down again. 'Tell me about your childhood. You said you lost your parents when you were seven. How did they die?'

Poppy looked down at her hands for a moment as she began folding and refolding her napkin. 'I never met my father. He deserted my mother before I was born. Apparently she wasn't good enough for him so he married someone else.'

'So your grandmother raised you?'

She nodded as she met his gaze again. 'She was wonderful, stepping in to take care of me after my mother died. I had a good childhood, all things considered. Lord Dalrymple was incredibly kind to me. He was a bit of a recluse but he always had time for me.'

'Were you disappointed he didn't leave you and your grandmother the manor as well as the dower house when he died?'

Poppy blinked at him in shock. 'Of course not. Why would we be? We weren't blood relatives. My gran was just his housekeeper.'

He gave a shrug of one broad shoulder. 'Your grandmother worked for him a very long time.'

'She loved working for him. She loved him.'

He arched an eyebrow. '*Loved* him?'

Poppy let out a breath in a little whoosh. 'I think maybe she did love him a little bit like that. Not that he would ever have noticed. He was living in the past, grieving for his dead wife Clara. But my gran never expected anything from him. She wasn't like that. It was a total shock to her when he left us the dower house. It was a nice gesture. It meant a lot to her. She'd never owned anything in her life, not even a car. She had grown up dirt poor and relatively uneducated. She'd been a cleaner since she was fifteen. To suddenly find herself the owner of a house was such a dream come true.'

'It must have been a shock to his family that he left the dower house to his housekeeper and her granddaughter.'

'Yes, there was a bit of a fuss over the separation of the deeds.' Poppy looked at him again but his expression was inscrutable. 'But Lord Dalrymple had made it clear in his will that we were to have it.'

'And then when she died her share of the house went to you.'

'Yes.'

There was a loaded silence.

'It's just a house, Poppy.'

She threw him a flinty look. 'It's not just a house. It's much more than that.'

'You can buy a much better place with the money I'm offering you. A place three times the size and with little or no upkeep.'

Poppy resented how he had gone from attentive listener to hard-nosed businessman in a heartbeat. She had been momentarily lulled into thinking he had a softer side underneath that ruthlessly tough exterior.

He was not soft.

He was as hard as steel and she had better not forget it. 'Why is the dower house such an issue for you? Isn't the manor enough? You have properties all over the globe. Why are you being so pigheaded and stubborn about a little dower house in a tiny little village in the English countryside?'

His mouth was set in an intractable line. 'I *want* that house. It belongs to the estate. It should never have been taken off the deeds.'

Poppy gave him a challenging glare. 'That house belongs to me. You can't have it. Get over it.'

His diamond-hard eyes bored like a drill into hers. 'Don't mess with me, Poppy. You have no idea how ruthless I can be if I have to.'

She got to her feet with an ear-piercing screech of chair legs against the floorboards. 'Get out of my shop.'

He gave her an imperious smile. 'It's my shop now—remember?'

Fury coursed through her body like a flash of hot fire. She wanted to slap him. She had never felt so tempted to resort to physical violence. She clenched her hands into fists, her body shaking with impotent rage. 'What are you going to do—charge me an exorbitant rent? Go ahead. Make me pay. I'll go public with it. I'll tell everyone you tried to blackmail me to sleep with you. I'll speak to every newspaper. Don't think I won't do it, because I will.'

He laughed, which made her all the more furious. 'I really like your spirit. No one has ever stood up to me quite like you do. But you're not going to win this. I *always* get what I want.'

Poppy glowered at him. '*Get out.*'

His eyes glinted at her goadingly as he leisurely got to his feet. 'Call the papers. Tell them what you like. They'll just think you're another wannabe gold-digger after money and fame. You'll be the one with mud on your face, not me.' He took out his wallet. 'How much do I owe for the tea?'

Poppy gave him a look that would have stripped graffiti off a wall. 'It's on the house.'

He held her gaze for a long, throbbing moment. 'I meant what I said about the rent. I don't intend to make any changes to the arrangements you made with John Underwood.'

She flashed him another caustic glare. 'Am I supposed to thank you? Kiss your feet? Prostrate myself before you? Go on, lay one finger on me and see what happens. I dare you— *Oomph*!'

His hands had grasped her upper arms so

quickly she didn't have time to do much more than snatch a quick breath before his mouth came down on hers.

It was a hard, possessive kiss, a hot fizzing pressure against her lips that made them tingle as if high-voltage electricity was passing directly from his body to hers.

Poppy had intended to fight him, but somehow as soon as his mouth connected with hers her lips softened and became totally pliant, melting beneath the fiery purpose of his. She opened to his command and tasted the full potent heat of him, the bold thrust of his tongue going in search of hers with erotic intent. He explored every corner of her mouth with spine-tingling thoroughness, leaving her breathless and barely able to stand upright.

But, even more *mortifying*, she gave a soft little whimper of approval just before he broke the connection.

It was of some slight consolation to her that he looked just as shocked as she felt. His eyes were almost black and a frown had appeared between his eyebrows as he dropped his hands from her upper arms and took an unsteady step back from her.

Poppy tried to think of something witty or pithy to say but her mouth was still hanging open in stupefaction.

He inclined his head in a formal nod, his expression now unfathomable. 'Thank you for the tea lesson. It was very…' He paused over the choice of a word. 'Entertaining.'

Poppy let out her breath in a flustered rush once he had gone. She knew the battle was far from over.

It was just beginning.

CHAPTER SIX

'I THINK YOU'RE being very pig-headed about this,' Chloe said a couple of days later. 'I keep thinking of that poor man starving up there at the manor.'

Poppy snorted. 'He's probably got a bevy of blonde bombshells to peel his grapes for him. Anyway, what's wrong with a microwave dinner every now and again?'

'I can't believe I'm hearing this,' Chloe said. 'You—the cooking-from-scratch queen of the kitchen.'

Poppy couldn't stop a reluctant smile from forming. 'I'm not averse to the odd bit of convenience food. I had baked beans on toast last night.'

Chloe covered her ears. 'Don't use such filthy language in my hearing.'

The chime on the door sounded and Poppy's

heart gave a little stumble. 'You get that. I've got to get the cookies out of the oven.'

Chloe snatched the oven mitts out of Poppy's grasp. 'He's not here to see me, more's the pity.'

'How do you know it's him?'

Chloe gave her a knowing look. 'Because you don't blush like a rose when anyone else opens that door.'

'It's only because I dislike him so much.'

'Yeah, and I hate chocolate.'

Poppy threw her shoulders back and walked briskly out into the tearoom. 'Good morning, Mr Caffarelli. Your usual?'

'I'm not here for coffee.'

She gave him a pert look. 'Tea?'

An enigmatic smile played at the edges of his mouth while her mouth tingled in memory of his hot, hard kiss. 'Are you free for dinner tonight?' he asked.

Poppy drew in a tight little breath as she put her hands on her hips. The hide of him! Where on earth did he get access to so much arrogance and confidence? Was it coded in his DNA? 'You don't give up easily, do you?'

'It's not in my nature.'

Chloe popped her head around the door. 'She'd love to go out to dinner. She's not busy. She hasn't been out on a date with anyone for more than three months.'

Poppy swung back and threw Chloe a livid glare. 'Do you mind?'

'What harm will it do to have a meal with him?' Chloe said. 'You know you want to.'

'I do not want to!'

'She *does* want to,' Chloe said with authority to Rafe. 'It will do her good. She needs to get out more.'

'I swear to God I'm going to—'

'So it's a date,' Rafe said. 'I'll pick you up at seven. I thought we could go to that new restaurant in the next village everyone is talking about.'

'I'm *not* go—'

'What should she wear?' Chloe said before Poppy could finish spluttering her protest.

'Surprise me.' He gave them both a smile and walked back out the door.

'You're fired,' Poppy said, flashing Chloe another deadly glare.

'You don't mean that,' Chloe said. 'Anyway, what could be more perfect than going to Oliver's restaurant with the seriously rich, staggeringly handsome Rafe Caffarelli as your date? How cool a payback is that? I wish I could be a fly on the wall when that two-timing pig sees you walking in on Rafe's arm. It's a perfect way to show him you're over him.'

'I didn't have to get over him in the first place,' Poppy said, folding her arms across her chest.

'Sure you didn't.' Chloe gave her another knowing look. 'You cried your heart out for a week. And you ate a whole cheesecake.'

'*Half* a cheesecake.' Poppy scowled at her. 'And I only cried because I really wanted to have someone in my life…someone to belong to. Ever since Gran died, I feel like I don't belong to anyone any more.'

Chloe gave her a big squishy hug. 'You belong to this village, Poppy. Everyone loves you. We're your family now.'

Poppy chewed at her lip as she walked back to the kitchen. Maybe Chloe was right—it would be a good way to demonstrate to Oliver she had moved on.

But Rafe Caffarelli?

He was crafty and clever. Everything he did was with a specific purpose in mind. She knew he wanted her house, but what if it wasn't just the house he had set his mind to possess?

Especially after that explosive kiss...

She refused to think about that kiss. She had tried to block it from her mind. Every time she thought of it she cringed at how *willing* she had been, almost desperate, practically hanging off him like a limpet, before he'd put her from him.

She couldn't make him out. He had bought her shop, yet he hadn't raised the rent and had told her he wasn't going to. Could she trust him not to suddenly change his mind? Was he trying to charm her by stealth?

He could hardly be in doubt of her attraction to him now. She tried her best to hide it but he was so damnably attractive! His casually tousled hair and the dark stubble on his jaw would have looked dishevelled or scruffy on someone else. On him it looked sexy and it made her fingers twitch to reach up and thread through those dark, silky strands or to stroke that chiselled plane of his jaw.

And his mouth… She gulped as she thought of the contours of his lips, how they were so finely sculptured and yet so utterly masculine; how he had tasted; so warm and yet so fresh. Would he kiss her again? Was that why he was taking her out to dinner? Would she have the strength of will to resist him?

Of course.

She'd been caught off-guard before. He had taken advantage of her momentary lapse of concentration. She would be better prepared this time. He could dazzle her with whatever strength of charm he liked.

She was back in control.

Rafe pulled up at the dower house just at seven. There was a cacophony of mad barking from inside the house as he raised his hand to the knocker. He heard Poppy shushing the dogs with limited success and then she opened the door.

'You look...' He was momentarily lost for words. 'Amazing.'

She was wearing a slim black cocktail dress that was simple but elegant, highlighting her trim figure without in any way exploiting it. The subtle sexiness was heart-stopping. Rafe swore his heart actually did miss a beat. She had her hair up in one of those artful twists that looked both casual and elegant at the same time. She had a simple string of pearls around her graceful neck and matching earrings, that he suspected weren't terribly expensive, but with her creamy skin as a backdrop they looked as if they had just come out of a bank vault. Her make-up was light and yet it highlighted every one of her girl-next-door features: the high cheekbones, the cinnamon-brown eyes and the perfect bow of her mouth, which had a fine layer of shimmery gloss on it.

He still couldn't get his mind to stop revisiting that kiss. It was on permanent replay in his head. He couldn't remember a time when a kiss had affected him so much. He had kissed dozens, probably hundreds of women. But something about Poppy Silverton's sweet mouth melting into his had sent an arrow of longing deep inside him that had nagged at him like a toothache ever since.

He wanted her. *Badly.*

'I'll just get my wrap and purse.' She ushered the little mutts back with a shooing gesture and bent to pick up her belongings from the hall table.

Rafe's gaze travelled the length of her legs, from her thin ankles encased in sexy high heels to the neat curve of her bottom. One of the little dogs—the one with a patch of black over one eye, like a pirate—growled at him warningly.

'Down, boy,' Poppy said.

'Are you talking to me or the dog?' Rafe asked.

A delicate blush bloomed over her cheeks as she put her wrap around her shoulders. 'Pickles is a little shy of strangers. But once he gets to know you he'll be all over you like a rash.'

'I can hardly wait.'

Her blush deepened a fraction. 'So…you like dogs?'

'I love dogs.' Rafe bent down and scratched behind Chutney's ears. Relish came over and pushed his mate out of the way to get in on the action, but Pickles was maintaining his beady-eyed stand-off, eyeing Rafe with the sort of suspicion a protective father might cast upon a suitor who had come to collect his teenage daughter for her first date.

'Do you have a dog at home?' Poppy asked.

Rafe straightened. 'No, I travel too much. It wouldn't be fair to leave it with household staff.'

'Where do you base yourself? Italy or France?'

'I have a villa in Umbria and one in Lyon. A have apartments in Rome and Paris I use for business trips. Our family owns a few villas in other locations around the globe. I won't bore you with listing them.'

She gave him a look. 'Which do you love the most?'

Rafe had loved the smallish but comfortable villa just outside Rome he and his brothers had grown up in before their parents were killed. Conscious of the extreme wealth she was marrying into, his mother had insisted on a more normal upbringing for her boys, reducing household staff to a minimum and even doing a lot of the cooking herself.

But his grandfather had sold the villa after

Rafe's parents had been killed. He hadn't consulted Rafe or his brothers about it. It had been delivered to them as a fait accompli. It had been devastating to lose not just their parents but their home as well. It was as if everything they had held most secure had disappeared. As a result Rafe tried not to get too attached to people or places or things. His brothers were exactly the same.

'I don't have a favourite,' he said. 'They each serve their purpose.' He held the door open. 'Shall we go?'

Rafe settled her in the car before he got behind the wheel. 'So, three months since your last date?'

'Chloe had no right to tell you that.'

'I'm glad she told me. I wouldn't want to be cutting in on anyone's territory.'

She sent him a narrow-eyed look. 'This isn't a date.'

'What is it then?'

She clutched her purse tightly on her lap. 'It's just a dinner between two…um…'

'Friends?'

'Associates.'

Rafe gave a little chuckle of amusement. 'I'm surprised you didn't say enemies. I must be improving a little in your estimation.'

'Not that much.'

'Come now, Poppy,' he chided. 'Let's not spoil our first date with bickering like children.'

'It's not a date!'

Rafe smiled as he pulled into a space outside the restaurant. 'Sure it's not.'

Poppy forced herself to stop scowling as she entered the restaurant with Rafe. She also had to stop herself from shivering in reaction when he put a gentle guiding hand to the small of her back. The electric sensation of his touch burned through the fabric of her dress. The sharp, citrusy scent of him made her nostrils flare. He was dressed in a dark-grey suit but he hadn't bothered with a tie. His shirt was a pale shade of blue, which brought out the olive tone of his skin. He was simply the most gorgeous man she had ever laid eyes on.

But it wasn't just his looks. It was the way he

carried himself that was equally attractive. He had a commanding presence, an aura of authority that made people stop in their tracks.

The *maître d'* was a case in point. Poppy watched as Oliver's new girlfriend Morgan practically swooned when she came over to greet Rafe. 'Mr Caffarelli, it's wonderful to welcome you here,' she gushed. 'We've saved the very best table for you.' She cast a cooler look towards Poppy. 'Hi, Poppy. How's the teashop going?'

'Hello, Morgan,' Poppy said. 'It's going just fine. We've been flat out just lately. I've been run off my feet.'

Morgan gave a tight smile. 'Come this way.'

Once they were seated at their table and Morgan had left them with menus, Rafe raised his brows at Poppy. 'Friend or foe?' he asked.

Poppy picked up the menu with a huffy shrug of one shoulder. 'I'd rather not talk about it if you don't mind.'

'Let me guess.'

'I'd rather you didn't.'

He leaned forward and pushed the menu she was using as a screen down with his index finger so he could mesh his gaze with hers. 'The guy who runs this place…Oliver Kentridge…he and you were an item, what, about three months ago?'

Poppy pressed her lips together without responding.

'And the Morag girl—'

'Morgan.'

'Sorry, Morgan—is the one who lured him away from you, right?'

Poppy let out a breath that sent her stiff shoulders down in a little slump. 'I don't think it's fair to blame Morgan for all of it. Oliver wasn't getting what he wanted from me so he went to her. If he cared about me he wouldn't have strayed. Obviously he didn't care enough.'

A little pleat of a frown pulled the skin together over his eyes. 'What wasn't he getting from you?'

Poppy shifted in her seat. This wasn't exactly the conversation one had in a public restaurant, was it? Not that anyone was sitting nearby, but still… 'Um…'

'Sex?'

She looked at his incredulous expression and

felt a blush steal over her cheeks. 'Why are you looking at me like that?'

'You refused to have sex with him?'

Poppy leaned forward and hissed at him, '*Will you please keep your voice down?*'

He leaned forward as well, resting his forearms on the table so his hands were within reach of hers. His gaze was very dark and very focused as it held hers. 'How long had you been going out?'

'A couple of months.'

His frown deepened. 'So what was the problem? You didn't fancy him or something?'

'I sort of did.'

'What does that mean?'

Poppy gave a helpless shrug. 'I think I wanted it to be more than it actually was… Our relationship, I mean. I was lonely after my gran died. I wanted to be with someone. I'd known Oliver for years. He was one of the guys I'd gone to school with. We had a lot in common, or so I thought. We both moved to London to do hospitality training. When he came back a few months ago we sort of got together.'

'So why didn't you sleep with him?'

Somehow one of his hands had found one of hers. Poppy looked down at the way his long, tanned fingers had curled around her lighter-toned ones, creating a circle of intimacy that would make any onlookers automatically assume their relationship was a sexual one. It made an involuntary shiver trickle down her spine. It made a liquid heat pulse between her thighs.

She took a scatty little breath. 'I wanted to wait a bit…'

'For what?'

'To see if the chemistry was right.'

'Clearly it wasn't.'

'No…'

The approach of Morgan with the list of the day's specials put a pause on the conversation. But, instead of leaning back in his chair, Rafe kept hold of Poppy's hand across the table. She was conscious of his warm, dry fingers curled around hers in an embrace that had an undercurrent of sensuality to it. She felt the slow stroke of his thumb against the underside of her wrist. It was a mesmerising movement that stirred her blood to fever pitch.

Morgan's eyes went to their joined hands before she addressed Rafe. 'Would you care for a pre-dinner drink?'

'Champagne,' Rafe said with an easy smile. 'Bring us your best.'

Morgan's eyes widened but she maintained her professional stance and nodded.

Poppy looked at him pointedly once Morgan had left. 'Champagne?'

He gave her a twinkling look that was devastatingly attractive. 'I finally convinced you to go out on a date with me. I think that's worth celebrating, don't you?'

'You didn't convince me.' She gave him a slitted look. 'You *coerced* me.'

He brought her hand up to his mouth, holding it against the slight graze of his newly shaven chin, causing a frisson of delight to pass through her entire body from head to toe. 'You wanted to come. Go on—admit it. You wouldn't be here now if you didn't. You would've found some excuse or slammed the door in my face when I arrived to pick you up. But no, you were ready and waiting for me.'

Poppy was annoyed with herself for being so predictable. Why *hadn't* she slammed the door in his face? 'I don't trust you, that's why. How do I know you're not going to suddenly change your mind about the rent?'

'Because that's not the way I do business.'

'But a teashop is hardly at the top of your list of must-be-acquired assets,' she said. 'It's nothing like your normal investments.'

'I'm all for a bit of diversifying.'

Poppy tried to read his expression but he was a master at keeping his cards close to his chest. She knew she was a novelty to him, hence the little quip about diversifying. She was probably the first woman who had ever said no to him. The trouble was she wasn't sure how much longer she *could* say no. Even now her eyes kept tracking to his mouth. She had felt his smile against the sensitive skin of her hand and it had set every nerve fizzing. What would it feel like to have that mouth press against hers again? Was that where tonight was heading?

Would he settle for just a kiss this time?

Would *she* settle for just a kiss?

Expectation, excitement, nervousness and anticipation were a heady mix in her bloodstream.

Would he expect *more* than a kiss?

There was no denying the chemistry that sizzled between them. It had been there right from the moment he had walked through the door of her tearoom. The problem was, what was she going to do about it?

Morgan came out with their champagne. 'So, what are we celebrating?' she asked as she popped the cork.

Rafe gave her another laid-back smile. 'Nothing special—just dinner between friends.'

Morgan's expression was sour around the edges as she directed her gaze to Poppy's. 'I didn't realise you moved in such elevated circles. There's been nothing in the press about you being involved with each other.'

Rafe's hand tightened warningly as it covered Poppy's. 'We're trying to keep a low profile. We'd appreciate your discretion.'

'Of course.' Morgan gave another one of her stiff smiles before she left.

Poppy glowered at him. 'What the hell are you

doing? She'll phone the nearest journalist and give an exclusive. I bet she'll even tell them what we ate and drank.'

'So?'

'*So?* How can you be so casual about this? You deliberately gave her the impression we were seeing each other. I'll be laughed at and mocked in the press. I'm nothing like the women you usually date. Everyone will make horrible comments about me and call me a gold-digger or something equally offensive.'

Just like they had done to her mother.

Poppy had found some of the news clippings in her gran's things after she had died. It had been devastating to find out a little more of her mother's back story. How a normal, mostly sensible girl had been lured into a rich man's world and dropped when she'd ceased to be of interest to him. Poppy was sure that was what had shattered her mother—the public humiliation of being rejected, discarded like a toy that no longer held any appeal. Poppy's playboy father had denied paternity when her mother had told him she was pregnant, and in those days it hadn't been as easy to prove or disprove as it was today when you could buy a testing kit online. Her mother had been painted as a social-climbing, gold-digging slut who wanted to land herself a rich husband.

Wouldn't the same be said about Poppy if she were seen in the press with Rafe Caffarelli?

'Why are you so worried about what people will think?' he asked.

Poppy chewed at her lower lip. 'It's all right for you. You're used to it. I bet hardly a day goes by without an article appearing somewhere with you at the centre of it. I hate having my photo taken even when I'm prepared for it. Some unscrupulous photographer will probably catch me off-guard with parsley stuck in my teeth, or without make-up, or dressed in my shabbiest tracksuit or something.'

He was looking at her with a smile tilting the edge of his mouth. 'I quite liked how you looked in that tracksuit the other night.'

'It had lint balls all over it.'

'I think you looked stunning in it.'

Poppy picked up her champagne flute for something to do with her hands. He was lethally charming in this playful, flirty mood. But she mustn't forget she had something he wanted—the dower house. He had tried other means to get her to sell it to him. Maybe this new approach was nothing to do with how attractive or unique or *cute* he found her, but rather another clever ploy of his to achieve his goal. 'I suppose you think that if you flatter me enough I'll change my mind and sell you my house?'

'I think you're mistaking my motives.'

She gave him an arch look. 'Oh really? So you're going to sit there and tell me you asked me out to dinner, not as a ploy to get me to change my mind, but just because you find my company scintillating?'

That sexy half-smile was still lurking around the edges of his mouth. 'I find your company electrifying. You're so unlike anyone I've ever met before.'

Poppy felt her belly do a complicated tumble turn as his wicked gaze held hers. 'I guess I must be even more of a challenge to you now.'

'Why's that?'

'Because I'm…you know…what I told you before.'

He cocked his head quizzically. 'What did you tell me before?'

Poppy blew out a breath. Did she really have to spell it out for him? She felt the heat of embarrassment ride up from her neck as the silence continued.

Finally, she let out a little breath and dropped the V-bomb. 'I'm still a virgin.'

CHAPTER SEVEN

RAFE PICKED HIS jaw up from the table where he felt it had dropped. 'Are you serious?'

'I told you before…'

'You told me you hadn't slept with your ex. You didn't tell me you hadn't slept with *anyone*.'

Her expression was defensive. 'Go on—call me a dinosaur. Call me a pariah.'

Rafe couldn't get his head around it. He had slept with dozens of women and not one of them had ever been without experience. Some had had much more than him, particularly those he had slept with in his teens.

He liked to think he didn't operate a double-standard; he liked to think he was as twenty-first-century, open and progressive about sex as everyone else. But something about Poppy's in-experience struck a chord of something terribly old-fashioned deep inside him that he hadn't even been aware of possessing until now.

A virgin.

In this day and age!

Rafe looked at her taking careful sips of her champagne, her toffee-brown gaze meeting his every now and again, as if she was trying to act normal in a totally abnormal situation. Or at least, it was abnormal for him.

He had the routine down pat: dinner and sex. It was a combo that always worked. He couldn't remember a time when it hadn't.

He always got the girl.

But Poppy Silverton was another story. From the moment he had walked into that tearoom of hers he had seen her as the enemy that he would eventually conquer, but somehow she had the edge on him now. It was laughably ironic. He was known for his steely determination, for his merciless intent, yet in this case he felt totally ambushed.

He had not seen this coming. He had been totally unprepared for it. She was the most fascinating and intriguing woman he had ever encountered.

And she hated him.

OK, so that was a minor problem, but he could work on that—get to know her, charm her a little and get her to feel a little more comfortable around him.

Get her to sell him her house.

That was still his goal. Nothing was going to sway him from it. He didn't back down from his goals, not for anyone. He wanted that house because without it the Dalrymple Estate would not be complete. He didn't do things in half-measures. When he set his sights on something he got it. It didn't matter what or who was standing in the way of it. The fact that a mere slip of a red-haired girl was standing in his way was immaterial. There had to be a way around this so he could win.

He always won.

Losing would be playing into his grandfather's belief about him—that he was not good enough, not strong enough to withstand the opposition. Vittorio had instilled in him and his brothers the sense that, like their late father, they were just paltry imitations of him. That *he* was the patriarch that no one could or would dare to outshine.

His grandfather's arrogance had fuelled Rafe's determination since childhood. It was like a river of steel in his blood. He abhorred failure. It was a word that didn't exist in his mind, let alone his vocabulary.

Rafe wasn't supposed to *like* his enemy. He wasn't supposed to respect her, or be intrigued by her, or want her like he had wanted no other woman. Desire was a pulsating force inside him even now. Just watching the way her lips cupped around the rim of her glass as she sipped from her champagne flute made him hard. He watched the rise and fall of her slim throat as she swallowed and wondered what it would feel like to have those rosy-red lips suck on him, to bring him to the brink of primal pleasure…

'So how did you get to the age of…?'

'Twenty-five.'

Twenty-five! He'd lost count of the number of lovers he'd had by the age of twenty, let alone twenty-five. 'How did you get to that age without having sex?'

'I didn't want to end up like my mother, falling for the first guy who paid her a compliment,' she said. 'I guess it made me overly cautious. I just wanted to be sure my first time was with the right person. It's not that I'm hankering after a wedding ring or anything. And it's not because of religious beliefs, although I have a lot of respect for those who have them.'

Rafe wished he could say the same. But the God of his childhood hadn't answered his prayers the day his parents had been killed. He had felt alone in the universe that day and the feeling had never quite left him. 'I don't think you're a pariah at all,' he said. 'I also think there's nothing wrong in being selective about who you sleep with. To tell you the truth, I wish I'd been a bit more selective at times.'

She gave him a tiny 'let's change the subject' smile. 'What do your brothers do?'

Making neutral conversation was good. *He could do that.* 'Raoul's involved in the family business on the investment side of things but he also runs a thoroughbred stud in Normandy. He's a bit of an extreme sportsman; not only does he ride horses at breakneck speeds, he's a daredevil skier on both snow and water. And Remy is a business broker. He buys ailing businesses, builds them up and sells them for a profit. He loves his risks too. I guess it's the gambler in him.'

'You must be constantly worrying about both of them. I'm almost glad I'm an only child.'

Rafe had survived the loss of his parents but the thought of losing either of his brothers was something that haunted him. They were both so precious to him. He didn't tell them—he rarely showed his affection for them, or they for him—but he would be truly devastated if anything happened to either of them. Ever since he was ten it had been his responsibility to keep watch over them. 'We each have our own lives. We try and catch up when we're in the same country but we don't interfere with what any of us is doing unless it's to do with the family business.'

'What role does your grandfather play in the business?'

'He's taken a bit of a back seat lately, which is

not something that comes naturally to him,' Rafe said. 'He had a mild stroke a couple of months ago. If anything, it's made him even more cantankerous.'

She looked at him for a little moment. 'You don't like him very much, do you?'

Rafe shifted his mouth in a rueful manner. 'I try and tell myself it must have been hard for him, suddenly being landed with three young boys to raise, but the truth is he was never really all that interested in us even before our parents were killed. My father and he had always had a strained relationship. But it got worse when my mother came on the scene. My grandfather didn't approve of my father's choice of wife. It wasn't just that my mother was French and lowly born. I think it was more to do with jealousy than anything.'

Poppy's brow lifted. 'Jealousy?'

'Yes, he hated that my father was happily settled with someone while his wife—my grandmother—was lying cold in her grave.'

'Did he ever see someone else or think about remarrying?'

Rafe made a little sound of derision. 'Oh, he had his women; he'd had them while my grandmother was still alive: housemaids, cleaners, local girls who he paid to keep silent with a few trinkets. He had them all from time to time, but what he didn't have was what my father had—a woman who loved him not because he was rich or for what he could do for her but because she simply adored him.'

'That's very romantic,' she said. 'How tragic they didn't get to have more years together.'

Rafe picked up his glass again. 'It was, but in a way it was better they went together. I can't imagine how either of them would've coped if they were the one left behind.'

A thoughtful expression settled on her face. 'Is that what you hope to find? A love like that?'

Rafe refilled both of their glasses before he answered. 'I guess I'll have to settle down one day. Sire a few heirs.'

'You make it sound rather clinical.'

'I come from a long line of Caffarellis. We're meant to marry and reproduce, ideally in our early thirties. It's a familial responsibility. Romance has very little to do with it.'

It had had nothing to do with his grandfather's marriage, which had been arranged by his grandfather's parents to increase wealth and possession of property. But, from what Rafe had gleaned from staff or relatives of staff who had previously been in the family's employ, it had been a miserable marriage from day one.

'So how will you go about selecting a suitable wife?' she asked. 'Check her teeth and bloodline? Conduct auditions to see if she knows what cutlery to use? Take her for a trial ride, so to speak?'

He chuckled as he lifted his glass to his mouth. 'Hopefully nothing quite as archaic as that.'

'So you plan to fall in love the old-fashioned way?'

Rafe studied her expression for a beat or two. Would he allow himself to fall in love? It wasn't something he had ever planned on doing. He didn't like getting attached to people. Loving someone gave them power over you. The one who loved the most ended up with the least power in the relationship. Falling in love was losing control, and the one thing he didn't like was losing control over anything, especially his emotions. Even during sex he always kept his head. He always kept a part of himself back, which was why that kiss had unsettled him so much.

Control was his responsibility.

Hadn't he spent his childhood protecting his younger brothers from the vitriolic and often terrifyingly violent outbursts of their grandfather? He had taken the verbal hits, and on more occasions than he liked to remember he had taken the physical ones as well. His grandfather's unpredictable temper and emotional outbursts had made his childhood and adolescence hell at times. It had been better once he and his brothers had been packed off to boarding school in England. At least then it was just the holidays Rafe had to keep his brothers out of the line of fire.

No, falling in love was not something he planned to do any time soon, if ever.

Morgan came over to take their orders for their meals. 'How's the decision making going?' she asked.

'I've decided,' Rafe said. 'How about you, *ma chérie*? Do you know what you want?'

Poppy's eyes widened momentarily at his endearment but she recovered quickly. 'Yes, the pork belly with fennel and lime.'

'And you, Mr Caffarelli?' Morgan stood with pen poised over the order pad.

'I'll have the lamb with redcurrant glaze and red wine *jus*.'

Once Morgan had left Poppy leaned forwards across the table again with a quirked brow. '*Ma chérie?*'

'It means "my darling".'

'I know what it means but why are you calling me that in front of her?'

'You don't like being called darling?'

'Not by someone who doesn't mean it.'

'I'm actually doing you a favour,' Rafe said. 'Think of what Morgan is relaying to your ex-boyfriend in the kitchen right now—here you are, out with one of Europe's most eligible bachelors. That's going to sting a bit, don't you think?'

Her scowl turned into a reluctant smile that made gorgeous dimples form in her cheeks. He suddenly realised it was the first time she had genuinely smiled at him. 'Maybe.'

'Were you in love with him?'

Her smile faded. 'I thought so at the time.'

'But now?'

She gave a little shrug of her shoulders. 'Probably not…'

'So you had a lucky escape.'

She met his eyes across the table. 'Thank you.'

'For what?'

'For making me come out tonight.' She twisted her mouth. 'For making me face my demons, so to speak.'

'You mean the one who's too cowardly to come out of the kitchen and say a simple hello to you?' Rafe said. 'Maybe I should think twice about asking him to cook for me while I'm staying at the manor.'

She jerked upright in her chair. 'You can't ask him!'

He picked up his glass and took a leisurely sip. 'Why not?'

'Because…because I'd like to do it.'

Rafe arched an eyebrow at her. 'You've changed your mind?'

She gave a little toss of her head, which made one of her curls bounce out of its restraining clip. She tucked it behind her ear with one of her hands. 'It makes sense, since I only live next door. Besides, he'd only be using my recipes. I might as well get the credit for them.'

'Indeed.'

'And I need the money.'

'Things have been pretty lean in spite of what you told Morgan, haven't they?'

Her brow crinkled in a frown. 'I know I'm not very good at the business side of things. Chloe's always telling me I'm too generous and give way too much credit to people who could pay if I made them.'

'So why a tearoom?' he asked. 'Why not a regular restaurant?'

'I knew I wanted to open a tearoom when I was about ten. My gran had taught me how to cook and I loved being in the kitchen with her. I thought I should do the right thing and get a proper qualification, but it was very different being in the kitchen in a busy Soho restaurant.'

'So you came back to look after your gran when she got sick.'

'Yes, and I don't regret it for a moment.'

Rafe couldn't help admiring her loyalty and devotion. It was so at odds with how he felt about his grandfather. He couldn't wait to get away from him, and loathed having to visit to fulfil his familial duty, such as for birthdays and at Christmas. He rarely spoke to him unless he had to. 'You must miss her.'

'I do…' She ran her fingertip round the rim of her champagne flute. 'Do you know what I miss the most?'

'Tell me.'

Her caramel eyes met his with deep, dark seriousness. 'Her chocolate brownies.'

Rafe blinked. '*Pardon*?'

She gave him an impish smile. 'Just kidding. I really had you there for a minute, didn't I?'

You had me the first moment I met you.

Hang on, what was he thinking? *Had him? Had him* in what way? Sure, he was attracted to her. What full-blooded man wouldn't be? But she wasn't his type. She was the homespun type. He was the hardboiled, been-around-the-block-too-many-times type. His world was of fast cars, fancy hot spots and easy women who knew the rules and always played by them.

Her world was a small, out-of-the-way village, baking cakes and scones and making cups of tea for lonely old gentlemen while waiting for Mr Right.

She was innocent and sweet; he was jaded and cynical.

It was a recipe for disaster.

'I miss her for her wisdom,' Poppy went on. 'She taught me more about food and cooking than any hospitality college could do. The thing most people don't get about cooking is it's not just a collection of ingredients, and hey presto, out comes a five-star meal. It's so much more than that.'

'So what does make a meal special?'

'The love that goes into it.'

'Love?'

'The best restaurants are where the chefs love

the food they prepare and the people they feed,' she said. 'It's a symbiotic relationship.'

'So what you're telling me is you actually love the people who come to your tearoom?'

She gave him a pert look. 'Maybe not *all* of them.'

Rafe laughed. 'So what do I have to do to win your love? Have my cake and eat it too?'

Her eyes narrowed. 'You don't want my love. You just want my house.'

I want much more than your house.

Rafe pushed the thought aside as Morgan approached with their meals. He had to stay focused. The goal was the dower house; that was what he was after. He didn't want or need anything else. He wouldn't be around long enough to invest in anything other than building a top-notch hotel that would make him loads and loads of money.

Goal.

Focus.

Win.

Sure, it would be fun to have Poppy Silverton in his bed for the short time he was here, but he wasn't about to offer her anything else. She was looking for her fairy-tale prince, someone to sweep her off her feet and carrying her off into a happy-ever-after sunset.

Rafe's princely attributes leaned more to the darker side.

That whole domestic scene women like Poppy were after was nothing like the life he had carved for himself. He didn't do picket fences, puppies and sweet-smelling babies. He was never in the same place more than a week or two. He never stayed with a lover more than a month; six weeks max. He didn't do commitment. Maybe he was more like his grandfather than he cared to admit.

Not evil, but not squeaky-clean either.

CHAPTER EIGHT

AFTER THEY LEFT the restaurant, Rafe drove Poppy back home and walked her to the front door of the dower house. She hadn't expected to enjoy the night out, but Rafe had been nothing but charming, and even though Oliver's restaurant wouldn't have been her first choice of venue, in the end it had given her a sense of closure.

But it niggled at her that yet again Rafe had achieved what he'd set out to achieve. He'd got her to agree to cook for him while he stayed on site at Dalrymple Manor. It showed how incredibly shrewd he was. He knew how to turn things to his advantage, to find an opponent's weak spot and then go in for the kill.

And she'd done exactly as he had hoped she would do. She had snapped up the bait and now was committed to seeing him every night as she delivered his food to his door. Was she so predictable, or was he particularly clever at reading her?

Poppy turned to face him on her doorstep. 'Do you have any preferences for meals? Any particular cuisine you'd prefer over another or are you happy with whatever I come up with?'

His dark eyes flicked to her mouth for a brief moment. 'That's not why I asked you out tonight.'

She arched a brow at him. 'Is it not?'

'No.' His voice seemed deeper than normal, almost husky.

Poppy's eyes were almost on a level with his as she was standing two steps above him, and she was wearing her highest heels. She could see the wide black circles of his pupils in those impossibly deep brown eyes. She could see the way his lips were pressed firmly together as if he was fighting some sort of private internal battle. She could sense the tension in him and in the fragrant night air that circled them. 'Then why?'

'I asked you out so I could sleep with you.'

Poppy's eyes widened at his blunt honesty. 'You don't pull your punches, do you?'

His mouth tilted wryly. 'Your honour is safe,

Poppy. I'm not going to have my wicked way with you tonight.'

'That's very reassuring.' It was downright disappointing, but to admit that to him would be rather perverse of her.

He captured one of her loose corkscrew curls and wound it round his finger, his eyes holding hers in an intimate lock that made the base of her spine tingle like sherbet sprinkled in a glass of soda water. 'I had it all planned. I was going to wine and dine you, flatter you with compliments and then bring you back here and have wild, bed-wrecking sex with you.'

Poppy swallowed a gulp. 'Y-you were?'

He unwound her hair and tucked it neatly behind her left ear as if she was about seven years old. 'You're a nice girl, Poppy Silverton. But here's the thing… I don't mess with nice girls.'

Mess with me! Mess with me! 'So…what changed your mind?'

'I've had more lovers than you've cooked hot dinners,' he said. 'I don't even remember most of their names.'

'I bet they don't forget yours in a hurry.'

He gave a rather Gallic shrug, as if to say that was just the way things were. 'I'm not what you're looking for. It would be wrong to give you the wrong impression or mislead you into thinking any alliance between us could turn into something more permanent.'

'You're surprisingly honourable for a playboy.'

He brushed the underside of her chin with his index finger in a barely touching movement that set every nerve alight with longing. '*Bonsoir, ma petite*.'

Poppy snatched in a scratchy little breath as she watched him walk down the path to his car. She'd been expecting another kiss. Her anticipation of it had been building from the moment they had left the restaurant. Actually, it had been building from the moment he had picked her up that evening and looked at her as if she had just stepped off a Paris catwalk. She wanted to feel that firm, cynical mouth pressed against hers again. She had been staring at his mouth all evening, wondering when he was going to do it. Maybe she should have taken matters into her own hands.

What would have been wrong with a quick peck on the lips to thank him for a lovely night out?

It wouldn't have been a quick peck, that was why.

Once his mouth connected with hers another explosion would be detonated, and this time one or both of them might not be able to step back. Hadn't she felt that simmering tension from the very first moment he had walked into her tea-room? She had never experienced anything like it before. It was a rhythm in her body that only he was able to set going. For all these years she had been waiting for the right man to unlock her senses. She had wanted to find someone who could make her heart race; someone who could make her skin sing with longing; someone who could make her sizzle with a desire so unstoppable it would totally consume her. Hadn't his potently hot kiss given her a taste of what he was capable of doing to her?

She wasn't without an understanding of the workings of her body. She had explored it and had been rather fascinated by how it reacted to stimulation. But she thought of sex as being like sightseeing—it was far more pleasurable to see the spectacular sights with someone else rather than all on your own.

He had said he wasn't going to act on his desire for her. Did he mean just for tonight, or never? She had seen the way his eyes had been drawn to her mouth time and time again, as if he was remembering how it felt beneath his own. Was he going just to ignore the pull of attraction that pulsed between them? He might have the strength of will to do it, but Poppy wasn't so sure she could. At least, not for much longer.

Chloe was agog when she came bursting through the door of the tearoom the next morning. 'Have you seen the paper?' She thrust a tabloid in front of Poppy. 'Everyone's saying you're Rafe Caffarelli's new love interest. That was fast work! I thought you didn't even like him. What the hell happened last night? Did you sleep with him?'

Poppy snatched the paper out of Chloe's hands. 'Of course I didn't sleep with him. I didn't even kiss him. We had dinner, that's all.'

She looked down at the society section Chloe

had opened. There was a photo of them sitting at the table last night. Rafe's hand was covering hers and their gazes were locked as if in a deeply intimate conversation.

'So?' Chloe prompted.

Poppy closed the paper and handed it back to her. 'So nothing.'

'Nothing?'

'Zilch.'

Chloe's brow was knitted. 'Not even a kiss?'

'Nope.'

'A peck on the cheek?'

'No.'

Chloe pursed her lips in thought. 'Did you have an argument with him or something?'

'No. In fact I agreed to provide meals for him while he's here.'

'Gosh, he must have really laid on the charm. I thought you would rather see him starve.'

'Yes, well, it was either agree to it or let Oliver do it.' Poppy tied her apron around her waist. 'Do you know Oliver had *my* passionfruit crème brûlée on the menu last night?'

'Did Rafe order it?'

'No, he doesn't have a sweet tooth.'

Chloe looked at her musingly. 'People's tastes can change.'

Poppy gave a little secret smile as she headed to the kitchen. 'We'll see.'

Rafe looked at the preliminary plans he'd drawn up but something wasn't sitting well with him. He couldn't put his finger on it. Normally he was so clear-cut on this stuff. He bought a property with development potential and sketched out plans to present to his design team to fine tune.

But this time something wasn't quite right.

The doorbell rang and he got up wearily from his chair. He'd lost track of time. He'd been sitting for hours going nowhere fast. He scraped a hand through his hair to put it in some semblance of order and opened the door.

'I have your dinner.' Poppy was standing on the doorstep with her three little dogs at her feet like miniature bodyguards. She was holding a tray in her hands from which delicious savoury smells were emanating.

Rafe had never seen a more beautiful sight,

and it had nothing to do with the fact that he was starving. ‘It smells divine,’ he said. ‘But it looks like you’ve got enough here to feed a football team.’

‘I wasn’t sure how big your appetite was.’ Her cheeks immediately turned a deep shade of pink.

‘Why don’t you join me?’ He pushed the door open a bit wider with his shoulder as he took the tray from her. ‘You’d be doing me a favour. I’ve been having one of those incredibly frustrating unproductive days. I could do with some company other than my own.’

She hesitated on the doorstep. ‘I wouldn’t want to intrude.’ She glanced at the dogs at her feet. ‘And I’ve got the guys with me.’

Rafe put the tray on the hall table as Chutney had already rushed up to greet him, wriggling his little body in glee. Relish was whining in delight in case he got overlooked. But Pickles, with his cute overshot jaw that looked like a drawer that hadn’t been closed properly, was eyeing him with that same beady look. However, Rafe thought he saw his stumpy tail wag just the once as he bent down to administer pats and scratches to the other two. 'The guys are more than welcome.' He finally straightened and met her gaze once he had closed the door. 'I guess you saw the paper? I think it was only in the one.'

She bit down on her lip and then released it. Rafe felt a punch of lust slam him in the groin. Her mouth was so full and ripe, so incredibly sweet. He had dreamt of those lips. It had kept him awake thinking how much he wanted to feel them on his again.

'Yes…' she said. 'But can't we make them retract it or something?'

He picked up the tray and carried it through to the kitchen. 'No point. They'd just make something else up. I ignore it mostly. They'll soon find someone else to target. Our "affair" will be tomorrow's fish-and-chips wrapper.'

'But I don't want people thinking I'm…you know…sleeping with you, when I'm not.'

He smiled down at her lopsidedly. 'Ironic, don't you think?'

Her big brown eyes looked up at him with a twinkle of amusement. 'Very.'

How was he going to resist her?

'Where would you like me to dish up dinner?' she asked, suddenly turning brisk and house-keeper-efficient. 'Lord Dalrymple used to take most of his meals in the morning room but I can set up here in the kitchen, or the formal dining room if you'd prefer.'

'This will probably come as a bit of a surprise to you but I can't remember the last time I ate in the kitchen,' Rafe said. Actually he could, but the memory of it was too painful to recall: his pretty mother, just two days before she had died, dressed in a flowery apron with a swipe of flour across one cheek as she'd bent down to offer him a teaspoon of thick, sweet cake batter to taste...

He pushed the vision away and added, 'It wasn't the way my brothers and I were brought up. Our grandfather didn't believe in fraternising with the domestic staff. Not in the kitchen at least.'

'He doesn't sound like a very nice person to me,' Poppy said as she set about laying the table in the kitchen.

Rafe watched as she set two places with the cutlery neatly aligned before turning to find glasses and napkins. She seemed to know her way about the place, but then he recalled she had spent a great deal of her childhood there. 'Would you like a drink?' he asked. 'I have wine, both red and white.'

She looked up from placing napkins on the side plates. 'Do you have lemonade?' But before he could answer she said, 'No, of course you wouldn't. It's far too sweet.'

'I have mineral water or soda water.'

'That would be lovely.'

Rafe wondered if she was avoiding alcohol in order to keep a clear head. God knew he should take a leaf out of her book. He was having trouble keeping his hands off her as it was. She was dressed in a cotton skirt that emphasised the slimness of her waist. Her three-quarter-length-sleeved sweater skimmed her small perfect breasts lovingly. She wasn't wearing much make-up—just a hint of shadow, mascara that made her lush lashes look all the more Bambi-like and a light shimmer of lip-gloss on her mouth. She was wearing ballet flats on her feet, making the height ratio between them all the more disparate. Her daintiness made him feel far more aware of his masculinity than any other woman he had ever encountered before.

The trouble was, he was feeling more than a little conflicted about acting on it. Would it be right to seduce Poppy, knowing he was not the man to give her what she was truly looking for?

A vicious war was raging inside his body. Desire wrestled with his conscience like they were two mighty, well-matched gladiators in a ring. His blood ran thick and strong with the need to touch her. Even the way she moved about the kitchen ramped up his desire to fever pitch.

Rafe fetched her drink and poured himself half a glass of red. 'So, what have you prepared for me?'

'I have a light starter, as I didn't want to overload your palate for the main course.' She put a pear, rocket, walnut and blue-cheese salad in front of him. 'It's a nice blend of flavours without being too filling.'

'It's delicious,' Rafe said after taking a few mouthfuls. But it wasn't the food that was so captivating. He watched as Poppy daintily speared a sliver of pear and popped it in her mouth. He had to drag his gaze away and, reaching for his glass, took a deep sip of his wine to control the rapacious hunger that was raging in him—and that had nothing to do with the desire for food.

'How did your family make their money?' she asked after a little silence.

'My great-grandparents on my father's side were property kings,' Rafe said. 'Farms, villas, hotels, businesses—you name it, they were in on it. They bought low and sold high. My brothers and I do the same.'

'Do you enjoy what you do?'

Up until spending such a frustrating day, Rafe would have answered an emphatic yes. But somehow today had made him question everything about his plans for the manor—even, to some degree, his plans for his life. 'Like any career there are good and bad sides to it,' he said. 'I love the challenge of finding a rundown property and following it through the various stages as it develops into a luxury hotel. But the hassles with local councils or development authorities can be incredibly tiresome.'

'Not to mention difficult neighbours.'

He gave her a wry look. 'I almost sacked my property manager over you.'

She looked aghast. 'Oh, surely not?'

Rafe twirled the wine in his glass, watching as it swirled against the sides in a blood-red whirlpool of contained energy. 'I'd seen Dalrymple Manor online and liked the look of it. James thought it would be a good investment. He did all the research and emailed me the photos of inside and I agreed. It had large acreage and the manor itself needed a rapid injection of funds to bring it to its former glory. It ticked all the boxes.'

'But?'

He met her eyes across the scrubbed and worn centuries-old kitchen table. 'There was an unexpected five-foot-five obstacle in my way.'

Her cheeks pooled with a light shade of pink, the point of her tongue sneaking out to deposit a layer of moisture across her lips as her eyes slipped out of reach of his. 'That would be me.'

Rafe felt a smile pull at his mouth. Of all the enemies he'd had to face over the years Poppy Silverton had to be the most delightful.

The most desirable.

'I think you're making a very big mistake with the manor,' she said. 'It's not cut out to be a playboy mansion.'

'Why do you think that's what I have planned for it?'

She gave him one of her cynical looks. 'You and your brothers have glamorous starlets coming in and out of your lives as if there are revolving doors on each of your bedrooms. Do they take a numbered ticket, like at one of those dispenser machines at the delicatessen, to see whose turn it is to warm the sheets of your bed?'

Rafe knew he and his brothers had been portrayed as having rather colourful lives. But what was portrayed in the press was just a fraction of the truth. Most of the time they spent working in hotel rooms on their own, trying to meet impossible deadlines, trying to please people who were impossible to please—most notably their grandfather.

Raoul compensated for it by taking life to the extreme. He set physical challenges that would make the average man shrink in cowardice. It was as if he had no fear. He had ice in his veins instead of blood. He didn't just stare death in the face every time he took on another seemingly insurmountable challenge—he laughed at it, *mocked* it. 'Take me down if you dare' seemed to be his credo.

Remy took risks that were more cerebral than physical, but no less terrifying. He won more than he lost, but Rafe worried that the day might come where fate would step in and make his youngest brother lose in a very big way.

Rafe threw himself into his work with a similar passion, but just lately he had become increasingly restless. He wanted more, but he wasn't sure what it was he wanted. He had money, more money than his father or grandfather had ever had. Even without the input of his younger brothers, he had built an empire that rivalled some of the most notable in Europe. If he never worked again his investments would see him out. But was it enough? What legacy was he leaving?

Who would he leave his wealth to?

Rafe couldn't stop thinking of Lord Dalrymple in his stately manor with no one but his housekeeper and her little red-gold-haired, fairy-like granddaughter to keep him company—and the greedy, grasping extended family waiting on the sidelines to get what they could for the place once he had died.

Had they ever visited him? Had they supported him after his wife had so tragically died?

'I don't plan to live here myself,' Rafe said. 'Once the redevelopment is completed I'll appoint a manager. I'll probably only visit once or twice a year after that. I have other projects to see to.'

'So I suppose Dalrymple Manor will be just another notch on your financial belt,' she said as she came around to his side of the table to clear his plate, her expression tight with disapproval.

'Here. Let me help.' Rafe rose from his chair but as he turned he suddenly found himself a whole lot closer to her than he'd intended.

She took an unsteady step backwards and he instinctively put out a hand to stop her from tripping. The sparks against his fingers where they were wrapped around her wrist were like little fireworks popping off underneath his skin.

He met her gaze and felt a stallion's kick of lust

strike him in the groin. He smelt her perfume; it was like a draft of some exotic potion that inflamed him with instant longing. He relaxed his grip, but as her fingers left his hold they moved softly across his palm in a trailing movement that made the blood roar through his veins. He felt a surge of lust-driven blood thicken him, heat flowing over his skin like the path of a flame.

Rafe slid a hand into the thick curtain of her hair, loving the feel of those bouncy curls moving against his skin like dainty, springy, fragrant blossoms of jasmine, each one caressing him, intoxicating him.

He would allow himself one kiss.

Just to see if it was as he remembered. Maybe he'd imagined the sparks of electricity shooting up and down his spine as his lips had come in contact with hers. Maybe her mouth would just be another woman's mouth today. It wouldn't make his head spin and his desire race like high-octane fuel through his veins.

He brought his mouth down within reach of the perfect bow of hers, taking his time, letting their breaths mingle.

'What are you doing?' Her voice was soft and husky, her warm, sweet breath dancing against his lips like a teasing spring breeze.

'What do you think I'm doing?' But before she could answer, or the controlled and sensible part of him could change his mind, Rafe did it.

CHAPTER NINE

POPPY HAD THOUGHT his kiss the other day was electrifying, but this time it was completely off the scale. As soon as his lips settled over hers it was as though fireworks had gone off under her skin. She had never felt such a surge of primal male energy before. It touched on something deep and essential to her as a woman. It was like breaking a secret code that had never been solved until now. Her flesh sang with delight as his mouth explored hers in intimate detail—the way his tongue came in search of hers in a brazenly, commanding gesture that had her belly quivering as soon he made contact.

She tasted the hot, hard, thrusting heat of him; tasted the hint of ruthlessness in his mouth; felt the chivalry in his touch that could so easily be put aside if the situation warranted it. It was that edgy, dangerous element about him that so totally captivated her. Hadn't she felt that from the first moment she had met him? He was a man who always got what he wanted. He didn't let anyone stand in his way.

His mouth ravished hers, plundering its depths with dips and dives of his masterful tongue against hers. Poppy shivered as she kissed him back, her tongue duelling with his in a heart-racing chase that made her toes curl inside her shoes. His mouth was hot, determined and purposeful, and she clung to him as she kissed him back just as passionately.

He gave a deep growl of pleasure and cupped her bottom in both of his hands, tugging her against the heated trajectory of his body.

Poppy slithered against him wantonly; her body aching for the pleasure his body was promising in that erotic embrace. She made a mewling sound beneath his passionate mouth, her arms going up to loop around his neck, to hold him to her.

For a moment she thought he was going to reach for her breast. She actually felt his hand move up her body, but then suddenly he broke the kiss and put her from him, moving some distance away as if he didn't trust himself not to reach for her again.

He scraped a hand through his hair and let out a colourful expletive. 'Sorry.' He was breathing heavily. 'I lost my head there for a moment.'

'Is that such a bad thing?'

He gave her a grim look. 'I never lose my head. *Ever.*'

'Maybe it's time you did.'

He shoved his hands in his trouser pockets and moved even further away, turning his back on her. 'This isn't going to work, Poppy. You know it isn't. It was a mistake to kiss you. I should've known better.'

Poppy felt herself bristling in affront. 'I'm not asking you to marry me.'

He turned and threw her a black look. 'You're not my type. Do I have to spell it out any plainer than that?'

Self-doubt crept up and tapped her on the shoulder, mocking her with its cruel little taunts: *you're unattractive. You're rubbish at kissing. You've got no pulling power, that's why Oliver and every other date you've ever had moved on to the next girl as soon as they could.*

Poppy straightened her spine and swung around to the door. 'I'll just get the rest of your dinner for you.'

'Forget about it.'

'It won't take a minute.' She turned back to look at him. 'I just have to dish it up. I won't stay, if that's what's—'

'I'm not hungry.'

She forced herself to hold his unreadable gaze. 'Will you be hungry tomorrow night, do you think?'

His eyes moved away from hers. 'I'll make my own arrangements with regards to food in future.'

'Fine.' She let out a stormy breath. 'I'll just get the dogs and be on my way.'

'So how did the meal go down last night?' Chloe asked the next morning. 'Did you tickle Rafe Caffarelli's tastebuds?'

Poppy kept her gaze averted as she went about getting the tearoom ready for business. She had used concealer that morning when she put on some make-up but it hadn't done much to disguise the stubble rash on her chin. It looked like she'd been scrubbing at her face with a handful of steel wool. 'There is something terribly defective about that man's tastebuds,' she said as she swished back the last of the curtains to let the watery sunshine in.

'But you didn't make anything sweet for him, did you?'

'No, of course not.' *Had her mouth been too sweet for him?* Poppy pushed the thought aside as she crossed the room to get the napkins out of the old pine dresser drawer. 'He's just one of those difficult to please customers we get from time to time.'

Chloe's gaze narrowed. 'What happened to your face?'

'Nothing, just a bit of an allergy,' Poppy said shutting the drawer firmly. 'I probably leant too close to the honeysuckle or something.'

'Since when have you been allergic to honeysuckle?' Chloe came over and peered at Poppy's chin like a scientist examining a ground-breaking discovery in the laboratory. 'You've got beard rash!'

Poppy jerked her head away. 'It's not beard rash.'

'It so *is* beard rash.' Chloe grinned at her. 'He kissed you, didn't he? What was it like?'

Poppy pursed her lips and started placing the napkins by each setting. 'I'd rather not discuss it.'

'Did he want to sleep with you?' Chloe asked. 'Is that why you're all uppity about it? Did he put the hard word on you or something?'

'No, he did not put the hard word on me,' Poppy said tightly. 'He told me kissing me was a mistake, or words to that effect.'

Chloe blinked. 'A mistake?'

'I'm not his type.' Poppy leaned over the table near the window to put the last napkin down and straightened. 'Not that I want to be his type or anything—it's just there's a way to let a girl down gently without savaging her self-esteem in the process.'

Chloe angled her head quizzically. 'So, let me get this straight: *you* wanted to sleep with him but *he* knocked *you* back?'

‘I’m not saying I would’ve slept with him, exactly…’

‘But you were tempted.’

‘A little.’

Chloe raised her brows.

‘OK…a lot,’ Poppy said as she exhaled a breath.

‘I expect he’s a very good kisser.’

Poppy’s insides gave a funny little tug and a twist as she thought about Rafe’s determined mouth on hers. ‘The best.’

‘Which you can say from such a position of authority because you’ve kissed…how many men is it now?’

‘Six…no, seven. I forgot about Hugh Lindley in kindergarten, but I guess a peck on the cheek doesn’t count.’

‘That many, huh?’

Poppy let out her breath on another long sigh. ‘I know, I know. I have some serious catching up to do.’

‘Maybe Rafe Caffarelli isn’t the right place to start,’ Chloe said, glancing at Poppy’s chin again with a little frown. ‘You could get yourself really hurt.’

Tell me something I don't already know. 'I'm not planning on going anywhere near Rafe Caffarelli,' Poppy said. 'He's made his position clear. I don't need to be told twice.'

A couple of days later a deafening clap of thunder woke Rafe up during the middle of the night. The wind whipped around the manor like a dervish. It howled and screamed around the eaves and rafters, making the manor shake and shudder as if it was being rattled like a moneybox.

He went over to close the window the wind had worked loose from its catch just as a flash of lightning rent the sky into jagged pieces. The green-tinged light illuminated the dower house in the distance. His stomach clenched when he saw that one of the branches of the old elm tree had come down over the roof, crushing it like a flimsy cardboard box.

He quickly threw on some clothes and found a weatherproof jacket and a torch. He pressed Poppy's number—his phone had recorded it when she'd rung about Chutney being missing—but she didn't answer. He didn't bother leaving a message. He snatched up his keys and raced out to his car, calling the emergency services on the way.

The wind almost knocked him off his feet. He hunched over and forged through the lashing rain, his mind whirling with sickening images of Poppy trapped under a beam. Which room was her bedroom? He tried to recall the layout of the house. There were three bedrooms, all of them upstairs. Wouldn't the main one be the one where the elm tree was?

He hammered at the front door once he got there. 'Poppy? Are you in there? Are you all right?'

There was no power so he couldn't see anything, other than when the lightning zigzagged or from his torch, which was woefully low on batteries. 'Poppy? Can you hear me?'

The sound of the dogs yapping inside lifted his spirits, but only just. What if they were all right but Poppy wasn't? '*Poppy?*' He roared over the howling gale.

'I'm up here.'

Rafe looked up and shone the torch at the pale oval of Poppy's face next to the gaping hole in the roof. Relief flooded him so quickly he couldn't get his feet to move at first. He felt like his legs were glued to the porch. 'I'm coming up,' he called out. 'Keep away from the beams. Don't touch any power outlets or wires.'

He picked up a rock, smashed the glass panel beside the front door and reached inside to unlock the lock. He went upstairs, carefully checking for live wires or debris, but it seemed the branch had cut cleanly through the old roof and done little else but let the elements in.

The three little dogs—even Pickles, the unfriendly one—came rushing up to him, whining in agitation and terror. He quickly ushered them out of harm's way into the bedroom on the other side of the house. 'Later, guys,' he said and closed the door before he headed to Poppy's bedroom.

Poppy was pinned against the wall near the window by the beam that had almost sliced her bed in half. Rafe's stomach pitched when he thought of how close she had come to being killed. She looked so tiny and frightened, her face chalk-white, her eyes as big as saucers.

‘Are you all right?’ His voice was hoarse from shouting.

‘I—I’m fine…I think.’

‘Don’t move until I check it’s safe,’ he said, shining the torch around.

‘I’m scared.’

‘I know you are, *ma petite*,’ he said. ‘I’ll get you out.’

‘Are the dogs OK?’

‘They’re fine,’ he said. ‘I locked them in the other bedroom.’

Once he’d established it was safe, he climbed over the fallen beam and grasped Poppy’s ice-cold hands. He pulled her close, wrapping his arms around her as she shuddered in reaction. ‘It’s all right,’ he said. ‘You’re safe now.’

‘I got up to close the window. If I hadn’t, I would’ve been right where that beam is…’

‘Don’t even think about it,’ Rafe said, stroking her back with soothing movements, trying to ignore the way his body was responding to her. ‘I called the emergency services on my way down. They should be here any minute.’

The sound of a fire engine and an ambulance

approaching could only just be heard over the howl of the wind. Rafe stayed with Poppy until the fire crew came up and led them to safety, along with the dogs, who were now safely on their leads so they couldn't bolt at the sound of thunder.

Once they were outside, Rafe draped his weatherproof coat around Poppy's shoulders. She was shivering uncontrollably but he had a feeling it was shock rather than cold.

'You'll have to spend the rest of the night some place else,' one of the fire officers said. 'That roof doesn't look too safe. Another gust of wind and the whole lot could come down.'

'I'll take her home with me,' Rafe said.

What did you just say? Are you out of your mind? It was too late to take it back, as the fire officer had already given a nod of approval and moved off to talk to one of the other officers.

Poppy glanced up at Rafe with a frown. 'I can stay with Chloe and her mother. I'll just give her a call…' Her face suddenly fell. 'Except my phone is upstairs by the bed.'

'It's two in the morning,' Rafe said. 'We'll sort

out more permanent accommodation later.' *You think that's going to happen once you've got her under your roof?* 'Right now you need a hot drink and a warm comfortable bed.'

He led her to his car, got her settled in the passenger seat and put the dogs in the back before taking his place behind the wheel. The voice of his control centre was still nagging at him like an alarm bell that hadn't been attended to: w*hat are you doing, man? Take her to a hotel.*

But somehow he managed to mute it as he turned over the engine and glanced at Poppy sitting beside him. 'All right?' he asked.

Her toffee-brown eyes seemed too big for her small white face. 'I think my phone is crushed under that branch.'

He reached over and gave one of her hands a gentle squeeze. 'Phones are easy to replace. They're a dime a dozen.'

She gave him a weak smile. 'Thank you for rescuing me and the dogs.'

He gave her hand a little pat before returning his to the steering wheel. 'Don't mention it.'

* * *

Poppy was still wearing Rafe's jacket as she sat at the kitchen table half an hour later, her hands cupped around a mug of hot chocolate. There wasn't a single tea leaf in the manor, not even a tea bag. The dogs were settled in the laundry on a pile of blankets Rafe had found. Pickles had even licked Rafe's hand instead of snarling at him.

'Do you need a refill?' Rafe asked as he came in from giving the dogs a bowl of water.

'No, this is perfect, thank you,' Poppy said. 'I'm starting to feel almost normal again.'

His dark gaze narrowed in focus. 'What's that on your chin?'

She put a hand to her face. 'Oh…nothing. Just a little allergic reaction…'

He took her chin gently between his finger and thumb. Something moved behind his eyes, a softening, loosening look that made her belly turn over. He ever-so-gently passed the pad of his thumb over the reddened area. 'I've got some cream upstairs to put on that.'

Poppy gave him a pert look to disguise her reaction to his closeness. 'I suppose you have to keep an industrial-size container by your bedside, along with a giant box of condoms.'

The edge of his mouth lifted in a wry smile. 'I only have three on me. They're in my wallet.'

'You surprise me,' she said. 'I thought you'd have them strategically placed all around the house.'

His hand fell away from her face, his expression becoming shuttered. 'The stuff you read about me and my brothers is not always true. We're not the partying time-wasters we're made out to be.'

'Haven't you heard the expression "no smoke without fire"?'

'Yes.' His eyes glinted as they came back to hers. 'I've also heard the one about playing with matches. Do I need to remind you of it?'

Poppy schooled her features into icy hauteur. 'Do you really think I would've slept with you the other night?'

'Undoubtedly.'

His arrogant confidence irked her into throwing back, 'I was interested in kissing you again, I will admit that, but that's as far as I was going to take it. But then, I suppose you assume every woman you kiss is yours for the taking. Obviously, I'm the exception to the rule.'

'That's something we could easily test—' he paused for a heart-stopping beat '—if you're game.'

Poppy didn't know if he was calling her bluff or not. Either way, she wished she hadn't been so foolishly reckless in brandishing about a self-confidence she didn't even possess. He had kissed her twice now and she had practically melted in his arms. What would another kiss do?

Make her fall in love with him?

She pushed her chair back and got to her feet. 'I'd like to go to bed.' She gave him a pointed look. 'Alone.'

'Wise of you.' He smiled a fallen angel's smile.

Poppy felt a shiver go down her spine as she thought of how that mouth had felt against hers, how his hard body had felt. He was sin and temptation wrapped up in one hell of a hot package. She was playing with fire, striking up a conversation with him, let alone anything else. She just didn't have the defences or the sophistication to deal with someone like him.

'Goodnight,' she said as primly as Mother Superior to one of her novices.

'Goodnight, *ma petite*.' He paused for a beat as his gaze held hers in a lock that sent a shudder straight to her core. 'Sweet dreams.'

CHAPTER TEN

POPPY DIDN'T EXPECT to sleep a wink with the wind still howling outside, but somehow the sound of rain drumming on the roof combined with the warm, cosy comfort of the bed in the Blue Room at the manor and the hot chocolate she had consumed was a somniferous cocktail that had her asleep as soon as her head touched down on the fluffy pillow. She woke to sparkling bright sunshine and that fresh, clean, washed smell of the earth that comes after a storm. She stretched her limbs and lazily glanced at the little carriage clock that was sitting on the bedside table.

Ten o'clock!

She threw off the covers and quickly threw her clothes back on. There wasn't time for a shower; she didn't have any toiletries with her in any case. She raced downstairs with her hair still awry when she encountered Rafe coming in from outside. The three dogs were at his heels, their tongues hanging out of the sides of their mouths as if they'd just run a marathon.

Rafe looked disgustingly healthy and fit, dressed in stone-coloured chinos and a white shirt, his hair brushed back, his jaw freshly shaven and his eyes clear. It was impossible not to feel a little dishevelled in comparison. Poppy knew her eyes weren't clear—she'd caught a glimpse of them in the mirror on the way down—and as for her hair… Well, the less said about that the better. She'd tried finger-combing it but it had been like trying to comb a fishing net.

'Good morning,' he said with irritating cheerfulness. 'Did you sleep well?'

'Why didn't you wake me?' Poppy asked, glowering at him. 'I should've been at work two hours ago.'

'I drove down and spoke to Chloe about what happened,' he said. 'She said to take your time. She's got things sorted at the shop.'

'I need to get home to shower and change.' Poppy pushed back her matted hair with an agitated hand. 'And I need to call someone about getting the roof fixed.'

'Already sorted.'

Her hand dropped back to her side. 'What do you mean?'

'I've called a local roofing expert,' he said. 'He's starting on it early next week.'

'*Next week?*' Poppy said. 'Why not this week? Why not *today?*'

He gave a loose shrug. 'Your roof was not the only one damaged by the storm. You'll have to be patient. Look on the bright side—at least you have somewhere to stay.'

'I can't stay here. What will people think?'

His dark eyes glinted. 'They'll think I'm being a very charitable neighbour in offering you a bed for as long as you need it.'

Poppy's eyes narrowed to the size of coin slots. 'You know darn well what everyone will think. They'll think it's *your* bed you're offering.'

He gave a disarming smile. 'You worry too much about what other people think.'

'I'll find a hotel.'

He hooked a brow upwards. 'With three dogs in tow?'

Poppy chewed her lip. 'Maybe you could mind them for a few days until—'

'No.'

'Why not?' she asked. 'They're following you around like disciples anyway.'

'I don't want the responsibility of looking after them,' he said. 'I sometimes have to travel at a moment's notice. I don't mind you being here with them, but I'm not running a boarding kennel. What if the roof takes longer than expected?'

Poppy could see his point. But if she were to find proper boarding kennels that would be another expense she could do without right now. How long before the village got talking about her sharing the manor with Rafe Caffarelli?

How long before the world got to hear of it?

'How long does the roofing guy say it will take?' she asked.

'A week or thereabouts.'

That meant two weeks staying with Rafe at Dalrymple Manor unless she could come up with an alternative. But what alternative accommodation could offer a kitchen the size of the manor? 'If I can't find anywhere else, is it OK if I use your kitchen while I'm here?' she asked. 'I do a lot of the baking for the tearoom at home.'

'Of course,' he said. 'It's not as if I'll be using it.'

Poppy worried her lower lip again. 'I know you said you'd make your own arrangements about food…'

'You don't have to cook for me,' he said. 'I won't be here for much longer in any case. I have other projects to see to.'

Poppy wondered if his other projects were female. She pushed her feelings of disappointment aside. It wasn't as if he was the man of her dreams or anything. She didn't even like him. Well, she hadn't up until last night, when he'd been so gallant at rescuing her, putting his own safety at risk to get her out. The way he'd held her in his arms and comforted her had made her feel so safe and protected…

She gave herself a good, hard mental slap. She had no right to harbour such whimsical thoughts. He was a player, not a stayer. Even if he did agree to a fling with her it wouldn't last more than a week or two. He had made it abundantly clear she wasn't his type. If he did happen to sleep with her, it would be for the sheer novelty of it. He'd probably joke about it with his brothers or friends in the future. How he'd found a home-spun village girl who'd never had sex before.

But then, why *wasn't* she his type?

It rankled that he had dismissed her so easily. She was female, wasn't she? Sure, a top modelling agency wouldn't be calling her any time soon for a photo shoot, but as far as she was aware she hadn't broken any mirrors just lately. What was his problem?

'What about rent or payment for board and expenses? How much do you—?'

'I don't want your money, Poppy.'

What do you want? The question was left unspoken in the silence.

Rafe undid a spare key from his keyring and handed it to her. 'I have a meeting in London this afternoon. I might not make it back until tomorrow or the next day. Make yourself at home.'

Poppy took the key and closed her fingers

around it as he moved past her. ‘Hey, guys,’ she called out to the dogs who were slavishly following Rafe. ‘Remember me? The owner who loves and feeds you?’

Their toenails clicked on the polished floor as they came back to her with sheepish looks and wagging tails.

‘Traitors,’ she muttered as she bent down to tickle their ears.

‘I’d love to have you and the dogs stay, but Mum’s allergic to dogs,’ Chloe said at work an hour later. ‘Anyway, why are you so against staying at the manor? You lived there with your gran for years and years.’

‘I know, but it’s different now.’

‘Yes, because you’ve got the world’s hottest, most eligible bachelor sharing it with you,’ Chloe said with a mischievous sparkle in her eyes.

Poppy frowned as she put on her apron. ‘It’s not what you think. Anyway, he’s not going to be there much longer. He’s off to London this afternoon. He has other fish to fry.’

'Are you sure about that?' Chloe asked. 'Anyone can see you two have a little thing going on.'

'We do *not* have a little thing going on,' Poppy said. 'I don't even like the man. He's too arrogant for my liking.'

'That's confidence, not arrogance,' Chloe said. 'He knows what he wants and goes out and gets it. And I reckon it's not just the dower house on his acquisition list. You're right up there at the top of his must-have items.'

Poppy shrugged off Chloe's comment. 'I don't think so. I told you before, I'm not sophisticated enough for the likes of him.'

'Ah yes, so you keep saying, but I was watching him when he came to see me this morning,' Chloe said. 'He was so concerned about what happened to you last night. I could see it in his eyes. I think he's more than halfway to falling in love with you. He just doesn't realise it yet. Maybe that's why he's heading back to town. He's trying to get his head around it.'

Poppy choked out a scornful laugh. 'Men like Rafe Caffarelli don't fall in love. They fall in lust and they just as quickly fall out of it, too.'

'Call me a hopeless romantic, but I think you're exactly the sort of girl a hardened playboy like him would fall for,' Chloe said. 'He hasn't been seen with anyone else since he met you. That's a bit of a record, since he usually has a new lover every week or so.'

'I bet the papers tell a different story tomorrow,' Poppy said. 'He'll probably have a couple of wild nights of sex with some glamorous starlet or model. He won't give me a second thought.'

Rafe called an end to the board meeting at six p.m. but his middle brother Raoul hung back to speak to him after the others had left. 'A no-show from Remy as usual.'

Rafe grunted. 'One day I'm going to throttle him, I swear to God. He could have sent a text or an email. Where the hell is he?'

'I think he's in Vegas.'

Rafe rolled his eyes. 'Let's hope it's a showgirl he's with this time, not sitting at a gaming table with a billionaire oil baron ready to toss for the lot.'

Raoul grimaced in agreement. 'Wouldn't be the

first time. Don't know how that boy wins more than he loses.'

'He'll lose one day,' Rafe said.

Raoul arched a brow in mock surprise. '*Lose?* That word doesn't exist in our vocabulary, remember? You've been drumming that into us since we were kids: goal. Focus. Win. The Caffarelli credo.'

Rafe frowned as he recapped his fountain pen. 'I worry about Remy. He's like a loose cannon.'

'You worry too much about both of us, Rafe,' Raoul said as he perched on the edge of the boardroom table. 'You're our brother, not our father. You don't need to take so much on your shoulders. Loosen up a bit. You seem overly tense today. What's happening with that dower house in Oxfordshire you were after? Have you convinced the owner to sell it yet?'

Rafe gathered his papers together with brisk efficiency. He didn't want to get drawn into any discussions about his private life, even with his brother. He'd only been in the city a couple of hours and all he could think of was getting back to the manor. He refused to acknowledge it was because Poppy was staying there.

He liked the place. It had a homely feel about it. He enjoyed the space and the peace of it. He wanted to keep working on the plans *in situ*.

'I'm still working on it.'

'I saw your photo with her in the paper a few days back,' Raoul said. 'She's not your usual type, is she?'

Rafe snapped the catch closed on his briefcase. 'Definitely not.'

'You looked pretty cosy in that restaurant,' Raoul said. 'You slept with her yet?'

Rafe's brow jammed together. 'What sort of question is that?'

Raoul leaned back as he held up his hands. 'Hey, don't bite my head off.'

Rafe clenched his fist around the handle of his briefcase as he lifted it off the table. Normally he would have no trouble with a bit of ribald humour between his brothers over his latest lover, but talking about Poppy like that felt totally wrong. 'I'm not sleeping with her.'

Raoul raised his brows. 'You losing your touch or what?'

Rafe gave him a look. 'So who are you sleeping with?' he asked. 'Is it still that tall blonde with the endless legs?'

Raoul grinned. Slipping off the desk, he punched Rafe on the upper arm. 'You got time for a beer?'

Rafe pretended to glance at his watch. 'Not today,' he said. 'I have some more paperwork to see to when I get home.'

'Home being where the heart is?' Raoul said with a teasing smile.

'You're a jerk,' Rafe said, scowling. 'You know that, don't you?'

Raoul dodged his older brother's playful punch. 'Always said you'd be the first to go down.'

'The first to go down where?'

'Down the aisle.'

Rafe felt his spine tighten. 'I'm not going down the aisle.'

'You're the eldest,' Raoul said. 'Makes sense that you'd be the one to set up a family first.'

'Why would I want to do that?' Rafe said. 'I'm

fine the way I am. I like my life. It's a great life—I have total freedom; I don't have to answer to anyone. What more could I want?'

Raoul gave a little shrug. 'I don't know… I've been thinking lately about what *Mama* and *Papa* had. It was good. They were so happy.'

'Hindsight is always in rose-coloured vision,' Rafe cut him off. 'You were only eight years old. You remember what you want to remember.'

'I was nine. My birthday was the day of the funeral, remember?'

How could he forget? Rafe had watched his brother bravely hold himself together as their parents' coffins had been carried out of the cathedral. Remy had been crying and Rafe had put an arm around him, but Raoul had stood stoically beside him, shoulder to shoulder, not a single tear escaping from his hazel eyes. He often wondered if the roots of his brother's death-defying pursuits had been planted that day. They were a way of letting off steam from all that self-containment. 'I remember.'

'You don't think they were happy?'

Rafe let out a breath. 'They were happy, but

who's to say what they would've been like in a few more years?'

Raoul shifted his mouth from side to side in a reflective fashion. 'Maybe…'

'What's brought this on?'

'Nothing.' Raoul gave a smile that looked a little forced.

'Come on,' Rafe said, putting his briefcase down again. 'Something's eating at you. You hide it from most people but I can always tell. You're like a Persian cat with a fur-ball stuck in its throat.'

'I don't know…' Raoul picked up a glass paper-weight and passed it from one hand to the other. 'I guess I've been thinking about things. I don't want to end up like *Nonno*. He has to pay people to be with him.'

'You've seen him recently?'

'I spent the weekend there.'

'And?'

Raoul lifted a shoulder in a non-committal shrug. 'It was sad…you know?'

Rafe *did* know. He had been having the same thoughts. His grandfather spent most of his time alone with just a band of people he employed to take care of the villa and his needs. It was a sterile life. There was no love or mutual enjoyment. His grandfather went from meal to meal with no real social contact, no real affection or connection. He got what he paid for: obsequious and obedient service.

'He's brought it on himself,' he said with the rational part of his brain. 'He's pushed everyone who cared about him aside. Now he has to make do with the people who will only do it for the money.'

Raoul put down the paperweight and slid off the boardroom table with a little frown. 'Do you ever think about it…about life? About what it's all about?'

Rafe hid behind his usual shop-front of humour. 'Of course I do. It's about making money and making love. It's what us Caffarellis do best.'

'We make money and have sex, Rafe. Love has nothing to do with it.'

'So?'

Raoul looked him in the eye. 'Do you ever wonder if the woman who is with you is with you because of who you are or because of what's in your bank account?'

Rafe felt an eerie shiver move over the back of his neck at the chilling familiarity of those words. Hadn't Poppy asked him the very same thing the first day she met him? 'Come on, man. What's going on?' he asked. 'Last time I looked, you were out there partying like the best of them. What's changed?'

'Nothing. But I've been thinking about Clarissa, the girl I've been dating recently.'

'You're *not* serious about her?' Rafe gave his brother an incredulous look. 'I admit she's attractive but surely you can do better than that?'

'It solves the gold-digger problem, though, doesn't it?' Raoul said. 'Clarissa wouldn't be marrying me for my money because her old man has plenty of his own and she's his only heir.'

Rafe picked up his briefcase again. 'One beer, OK? After that I have to get going.'

CHAPTER ELEVEN

POPPY WAS IN the smaller of the two sitting rooms, wiping copious tears from her eyes as the credits rolled on one of her favourite classic romance movies, when Rafe suddenly appeared in the doorway.

'What's wrong?' he asked, frowning as he came towards her. 'Why are you crying? Has something happened?'

Poppy sprang off the sofa guiltily. She stuffed her sodden tissue up the sleeve of her pink teddy-bear pyjamas and wished she didn't have a red nose and red eyes to match her cheeks, not to mention her hair. 'It's just a movie. I always cry even though I've watched it about a gazillion times.'

He bent down and picked up the DVD case. '*An Affair to Remember*... I don't think I've seen that one. What's it about?'

'It's about a spoilt, rich playboy who meets this girl on a cruise…' Poppy felt her blush deepen. 'Never mind. You wouldn't like it. It was made decades ago. I bet you only like movies with lots of car chases and heaps of CGI and over-the-top action.'

He put the case down again, his expression unreadable. 'I didn't think you'd still be up. It's almost one in the morning.'

'I had to bake some extra things for one of my customers,' Poppy said. 'She's having some guests over for a dinner party tomorrow. I made the desserts for her.'

'That's sounds like a good little money-spinner for you.'

Poppy averted her gaze as she popped the DVD back in its case and clicked it shut. 'I wasn't expecting you back tonight. I thought you'd make the most of the nightlife in London while you were there.'

'After my meeting I had a quiet beer with my middle brother, Raoul.'

'So, no hot date or shallow pick-up?'

'No.'

'You must be losing your touch.'

His look was unreadable. 'That's what my brother said.'

There was a little silence.

'You do charge people for cooking those extras, don't you?' he asked.

Poppy blew out a little breath. 'I always say I'm going to…'

'But you're trying to run a business, for God's sake,' he said. 'Your goal is to make a profit. That should be your focus, not trying to be everyone's best friend.'

'I know, I know. Do you think I haven't been told this a hundred times?'

'Do you want me to help you?' he asked. 'I can have a look over your books. I can see where the leaky holes are and put the necessary plugs in place. You won't have to lose any sleep or friends over it.'

She looked up at him gratefully. 'Would you do that?'

He gave her a slow smile that made her legs go weak. 'I'd be glad to.'

Another little silence fell between them.

Poppy hugged her elbows with her crossed over arms. 'It's been funny being here tonight—funny weird, not funny hilarious.'

'Why?'

'Because I spent so much of my childhood here, right in this room. Lord Dalrymple let Gran and me use it. He said it was because the television reception was better here than at the dower house, but I think he liked having us around in the background.' She gave a little sigh. 'This is the first time I've been in here since Gran died.'

He came over and placed his hands gently on the tops of her shoulders. 'I should've realised it might be tough coming back here. I should have postponed my meeting and stayed with you.'

Poppy looked up into his deep, dark eyes. He was standing very close; close enough to smell the citrus base of his aftershave and the hint of late-in-the-day male sweat that was equally intoxicating. 'I don't need babysitting.'

A corner of his mouth lifted in a wry smile. 'So says the pint-sized girl who's wearing pink teddy-bear pyjamas, and hippopotamus slippers on her feet.' One of his hands moved from her shoulder to cup the nape of her neck. 'Which should be enough to stop me doing this.'

She swallowed. 'Doing…what?'

His mouth came down towards hers. 'I think you know what.'

'I thought you said you didn't want to…?'

He pressed a soft-as-air kiss to her lips. It barely touched her but it set every nerve longing for more. 'I want to,' he said in a rough, sexy tone. 'I want to very much. I've thought of nothing but you the whole time I was in London. How you taste, how you smell, how you feel.'

Poppy's breath hitched on something sharp in her chest as his mouth came back down to hers. The kiss was longer this time and deeper. She felt the first brush-stroke of his tongue against her mouth and her spine liquefied. She opened to him on a little whimper of approval, her hands winding up around his neck, her body pressing closer to the hard warmth of his.

His tongue played with hers, cajoling it into a dance that was brazenly erotic. He moulded her to him, his hands pressing against her bottom to hold her against his aroused body. He felt so thick and strong pulsing there against her neediness. The empty, achy feeling inside her was almost unbearable, especially when the answer to it was so temptingly close.

He broke the kiss to move his lips down to the side of her neck where a thousand nerves were trembling in anticipation. 'You should tell me to stop before this gets out of hand.'

'What if I don't want you to stop?' She angled her neck to give him better access.

He framed her face in his hands, looking deep into her passion-glazed eyes. 'I could hurt you.'

Her heart kicked against her ribcage at the concern in his gaze. 'I'm sure you won't.'

He leaned his forehead against hers, his warm breath mingling intimately with hers. 'This is crazy…' He drew in a breath as if to steady himself. 'Everything about this is crazy.'

'I feel a little crazy around you,' Poppy confessed as she planted a soft, teasing kiss to his mouth.

He kissed her back, a light play of his lips upon

hers, pressing, nibbling, caressing. 'Do you have any idea how out of my depth I'm feeling right now?'

She gave him a wry look. 'Isn't that what I'm supposed to be feeling?'

He cupped her face in his hands again. 'How *do* you feel?'

Poppy shivered as his dark eyes centred on her mouth. 'Nervous, excited… A little worried I might disappoint you…'

His gaze held hers with a look that was surprisingly tender. 'You have no need to be worrying about that. This first time is all about you. I don't want you to feel concerned about anything else but your needs.'

Poppy touched his lower lip with the tip of her finger. 'I do know what an orgasm is. I've had them…you know…? By myself…'

His eyes darkened. 'Do you want to show me what works for you or would you prefer me to discover it for myself?'

Poppy felt a hot blush storm into her cheeks. 'I think I'd feel more comfortable with you discovering it…'

His thumbs stroked her cheeks in a slow and gentle caress. ‘Making love with someone for the first time is all about discovering what works and what doesn’t. I want you to tell me if you want to stop at any point. If you don’t feel comfortable then we can call a halt. You’re the one in control, OK?’

Poppy wondered if she could have chosen a better first lover. He seemed so concerned for her, so adamant that she was not to be pressured or frightened or pushed out of her depth. For someone with such a racy reputation, he was showing a softer, gentler side that was powerfully seductive. She wanted to melt into his hard male body, to lose herself in his sensual expertise.

She didn’t want to think about the dozens of women who had been with him before. In a strange way, it felt as if it was the first time for both of them. She felt it in the slight hesitancy of his touch, the way his hands moved over her in almost reverent discovery. Like how he explored her breasts, as if they were the most precious, sensitive globes he had ever touched.

She shuddered as he slid his hand under her pyjama top, shaping her, the warm cup of his palm making every hair on her head tingle at the roots. He brushed the pad of his thumb over her tight nipple and a shower of sensation cascaded down her spine. A hot spurt of longing fired between her legs and she pressed herself closer, wanting more of him, wanting his skin on her skin without the frustrating barrier of their clothes.

His mouth covered hers in a searing kiss; it burned and sizzled every nerve-ending until she was breathless. He pushed aside her pyjama top as if it was nothing more than a scrap of tissue paper, his hand cupping and shaping her possessively as his mouth bewitched hers. She felt the drag of desire deep and low in her belly, the slow but delicious ache that tugged and pulled, drawing her towards him like a magnet. Her loins pulsed and ached with the need for more. She pressed herself even closer, her insides melting as she felt the hard, insistent press of his body against her.

He brought his mouth to her breast in a hot, moist caress that made her quake with desperate need. His tongue laved her tightly budded nipple, playing with it, teasing it, tantalising it until she was whimpering in soft little gasps of want.

'Not here,' he said. 'We need a bed.'

Poppy's breath came out in a startled whoosh as he scooped her up in his arms. 'I'm too heavy to carry upstairs.'

'You're a featherweight. I'm twice the weight of you. I'm worried I'm going to crush you.'

Poppy had never felt more feminine in her life. She wrapped her arms around his neck and gave herself up to the thrill of being swept off her feet. Each step he took on the staircase made her heart thump harder. It was one step closer to him taking her into his full possession. Her skin danced with the anticipation of it, every nerve in her body alert and finely tuned to the radar of his.

It seemed like for ever yet it was no time at all before her back was pressed against a firm mattress. He came down over her, his mouth hot and insistent on hers, his hands moving over her in gentle caresses that peeled off her night clothes with a slow deliberation that made her blood tingle in her veins. She reached for his shirt buttons, undoing them with fevered concentration.

She wanted to kiss every inch of his hot flesh, to feel it shiver and shudder under the ministrations of her lips and tongue.

He shrugged off his shirt as her hands reached up to explore the carved muscles of his chest and shoulders. 'You work out.'

'A bit.' His mouth found the underside of her breast, his lips moving lightly over the sensitive skin like a maestro with an instrument he has never played before. 'You are so beautiful.'

The hot press of his naked chest against hers made her body react like a wanton. Her bones melted, her limbs unhinged, her spine loosened. She ran her hands over his taut buttocks, pressing him against her need, wanting to feel the hot, hard probe of his flesh in her aching centre. She went for his buckle and blindly unfastened it as her mouth met his in a fiery kiss. She felt him against her, so erect, so ready for her it made her insides shift like tectonic plates beneath the earth. She touched him through the fabric of his trousers, stroking the thick length of him while his tongue played with hers.

He briefly broke the kiss so he could shuck off

his trousers and underwear. Poppy faintly registered the thud of his shoes hitting the floor. She was mesmerised by the male beauty of his body. It wasn't that she hadn't seen a naked man before but she had never seen one who looked so magnificent. She touched his tanned flat abdomen with an experimental glide of her hand. 'You're so…' she swallowed convulsively '…big.'

'Don't be frightened, *ma belle*.' He took her hand and placed it against his erection. She wrapped her fingers around him, getting to know his shape and feel. He was both satin and steel, power and potency, yet vulnerable too. She felt the pulse of his blood against her hand, the need there thundering so similarly to what was happening in her own body. There was even a bead of moisture forming at the head of his erection; just like the slippery dew she could feel secretly gathering between her thighs.

He gently pulled her hand away and pressed her back down against the mattress, his limbs in a sexy tangle with hers. 'My turn to explore you.' He laid a hand on her belly, just above her pubic bone.

Poppy shivered at the intimate contact; those long fingers were *so close* to where she most ached and throbbed. Her breath caught in her throat as he gently separated her with his fingers as if she was a delicate hothouse flower that needed careful handling. Her nerves quivered and shook as he delicately traced her form, not touching her anywhere too hard or for too long, his slow but sure process building up a delicious tension inside her.

'I want to taste you.'

Poppy saw the intent in his coal-black eyes and shuddered in nervous anticipation. She felt him move down her body, his warm breath caressing her folds, his tongue stroking the seam of her body in a gentle sweep that had her sucking in a sharp breath and shrinking back in startled surprise. 'Oh!'

He paused. 'Don't back away from it, *ma petite*. Relax; let yourself go.'

'I don't think I can…' Poppy suddenly felt exposed and inadequate. What if she was hopeless at this? What if he thought she was ugly or different down there? She hadn't waxed as neatly as her peers. She found the thought of being totally bare down there a little unsettling. Was she supposed to look like a little girl or a woman? What did men want? Was he comparing her to all his other lovers?

'Hey.' Rafe captured her chin and made her look at him. 'You're beautiful. You taste beautiful. You smell beautiful.'

Poppy covered her face with her hands. 'This is why I'm still a virgin at twenty-five. I'm hopeless at this.'

He tugged her hands away from her face. 'You're not hopeless at this. Relax, *ma petite*. We're not in a hurry. Take all the time you need.'

'But what about you?'

He stroked the flank of her thigh with a slow, caressing touch. 'I can come in two minutes or forty-two. It's in my control.'

She frowned. 'But I thought…'

He pressed the pad of his thumb over her lips. 'Stop thinking, *ma chérie*. Your job right now is to feel.'

Poppy let out an uneven breath as he stroked her thigh again. His touch was like a velvet glove against her skin. She closed her eyes and gave herself up to the moment, to the feel of his hand on her thigh, her belly and her breasts in gentle glides that were almost reverent. He came back to her with his mouth, soft as a feather landing on her, waiting for her to feel comfortable before progressing to firmer, more intimate caresses. She felt the slow stroke of his tongue, the sensations ricocheting through her, but instead of fighting them this time she embraced them. It was like a giant wave coming down over her. It swept her up in its vortex, tumbling her over and over in a dizzying whirlpool that made her feel disoriented. She heard a high, keening cry split the air and realised with quite some embarrassment that it had come from her.

It sounded so primal, *so carnal.*

He brushed the damp hair away from her forehead, a smile that was just shy of smug playing at the edges of his mouth. 'See? You're not hopeless at this. You're a natural.'

Poppy trailed a fingertip down his sternum rather than meet his triumphant gaze. 'So…forty-two minutes, huh? Did you set a stop-watch or something?'

He pushed her chin up so her gaze was level with his. 'Being a considerate lover is a responsibility I take very seriously as a man. No woman should feel rushed to meet a timetable that isn't hers. Your body will have different moods and needs. What works well one time may not work so well another time.'

Poppy traced her index finger over the contour of his lower lip, her softer skin catching on his stubble like silk on sandpaper. 'You seem to know your way around a woman's body.'

'I'm still getting to know yours but what I've discovered so far is delightful.' He captured her fingertip with his lips and sucked it into his mouth. She shivered as she felt the intimate pull of his warm mouth, his eyes glittering with primal intent as they held hers.

Poppy sank back with a blissful sigh as he moved over her, balancing his weight on his arms so as not to crush her. The sexy abrasion of his masculine leg hair against her smoother skin was a potent reminder of how different he was from her. His mouth covered hers in a sizzling-hot kiss that fired up all of her nerve-endings all over again. His tongue played with hers in a commanding way, taming hers into submission, then backing off, making her come in search of him, encouraging her to be bolder, more daring. She took up the challenge, enjoying the deep murmurs of approval that came from his throat as her tongue danced with his.

His hands glided over her breasts, touching, teasing in unhurried strokes that made her heart race. He worked his way down her abdomen, those lazy caresses over her belly, hips and thighs making her skin tremble all over with need. She felt his erection move against her and got a sense of the urgency that was building in him from the increased rate of his breathing. It excited her that she was the one doing that to him, that she could have that sensual power over him.

He reached for a condom from the bedside drawer and tore the little packet with his teeth before applying it. He was not only a sensitive lover, but also a safety-conscious one. How different from her mother's experience with her father, who had only wanted to slake his lust without a thought for the consequences.

'Are you still sure you want to go ahead with this?' Rafe asked.

Poppy touched his steely length, her body already pulsing with a longing so intense it was like a pain deep inside. 'I want you to make love to me.'

His eyes meshed with hers for a long moment of intimacy that made her feel as if she was the only woman in the world he had ever wanted or would ever want. 'I'll go really slowly,' he said in a gravel-rough voice. 'Tell me if I'm hurting you.'

She put her arms around his neck and kissed his mouth, breathing in the male scent of him, the raspy feel of his stubble on her softer skin making her celebrate her femininity in a way she had never done before.

He moved against her, guiding himself as he gently nudged her apart. 'All right so far?'

Poppy nodded. 'I'm OK.'

'Relax, *ma petite*.' He waited for her to let go of her tight muscles before he tried again. 'You're in control, remember?'

She felt the glide of his body within hers, her own moisture making the passage far easier than she had thought possible. He was so big, yet her body stretched to accommodate him. She was feeling really proud of herself, but then he went that little bit deeper and a sharp pain tugged at her. 'Ouch!'

He stopped and held her steady, his deep-brown eyes full of concern. 'Sorry, *ma chérie*. That was too deep, yes?'

'No…I'm OK.' She took a little breath. 'I'm sorry for being such a drama queen.'

'You're not being a drama queen.' He brushed the hair back from her forehead. 'You're tiny. Just try not to tense up. Your muscles need to be relaxed to accommodate me. Let your legs go.' He kissed her softly on the mouth, making her melt into him as he slowly went deeper. Her tender flesh caught on him but it didn't hurt as much this time. She lifted her hips and he went in with a smooth, gliding thrust that made her gasp in pleasure.

He paused again. 'All right?'

'Mmm…' Poppy caressed his back and shoulders, getting used to the feel of him deep inside her. He started to thrust, the friction of his body within hers stirring sensations that spiralled out from her core. She felt the tight ache of want building inside her; it was a thrumming pulse that reverberated throughout her body.

Taking his cue from her, he gradually increased his pace, using his fingers to enhance her pleasure. She felt the exquisite goal approaching but it was just out of her reach. She shifted restlessly against him. 'I'm sorry. I can't do it.'

'Shhh,' he soothed her gently. 'Take all the time you need. I'm not going anywhere.'

Poppy gave herself up to his slowly measured thrusts, each one deeper and more exquisite than the one before. He caressed her intimately, varying the speed and pressure until she was hovering on the edge of a scarily high precipice.

'Go with it, *ma petite*,' he coaxed her gently. 'Don't hold back from it.'

Poppy gasped as the first wave of her orgasm smashed into her. She felt stunned by the velocity of it. It was like being on an out-of-control fairground ride. She was spinning around and around; she didn't know which way was up or which way was down. Every cell of her body seemed to be concentrated at that one point in her body. She threw her head back against the pillows as the sensations coursed through her. It went on and on, thrashing her about until she felt like she was being shaken alive.

He waited until she was coming out of it to take his own pleasure. She felt the increase of tension in him, felt the bunching of his muscles underneath her hands as he pitched himself into oblivion with a deep groan that was thrillingly, unmistakably male.

There was a long moment of silence.

Poppy wasn't sure what to say. What did you say after the most stunning experience of your life? 'Thanks' didn't seem quite appropriate somehow. Her emotions were scattered like the pieces of a jigsaw puzzle that had been shoved out of place. She didn't know what to think or feel. He had been so tender with her, so caring and considerate. How could she have thought she hated him? Her feelings were a little closer to the other end of the spectrum, but she didn't want to think about that right now. Falling in love with someone just because they were a fabulous lover wasn't a good enough reason, in her opinion. Loving someone had more to do with having similar values, and trust and commitment on both sides; knowing they would always be there for you, no matter what. Rafe Caffarelli wasn't making those sorts of promises. This was a fling and the sooner she got her head—and her body—around it the better.

He propped himself up again to look down at her. 'How do you feel?'

Poppy felt a little tug on her heart at the tender concern she could see in his gaze. 'I'm fine,' she said. 'No worse for wear…I think.'

He picked up one of her stray curls and tucked it behind her ear. 'You were amazing.'

She gave him her version of a worldly look. 'I bet you say that to all the girls.'

A frown pulled at his brow. 'I know you probably won't believe this, but it was different for me.'

'How?'

'Just…different.'

Poppy searched his features for a moment. 'I thought you were pretty amazing too.'

He gave her a slow smile that made her insides melt all over again. 'It's not like you have anyone to compare me to.'

'Not yet.'

His brows snapped together as he moved away and disposed of the condom. His movements seemed almost too controlled, stiff almost, as if he was trying to contain his emotions and not quite managing it. 'I might be a playboy, but I insist that my partners—no matter how temporary—are totally exclusive.'

Poppy sat up and hugged her knees to cover her nakedness. 'Touchy.'

He threw her a hard little glare. 'I mean it, Poppy. I am not unfaithful in my relationships and I won't tolerate it in a partner.'

'*Am* I a partner?'

He drew in a breath and released it in a rush as if he had come to a decision in his mind. 'You are now.'

'For how long?'

His eyes met hers, searing hers with hot longing and unbridled lust. 'This will burn itself out,' he said. 'It always does.'

'Give me a ballpark figure,' Poppy said. 'A week? A month?'

'I'm not planning on being down here for too much longer.' He scraped a hand through his hair to push it back off his forehead. The sexily tousled look made him look even more staggeringly gorgeous. 'And I'm not a great believer in long-distance relationships.'

She rested her chin on the top of her bent knees as she wrapped her arms around her ankles. 'I guess you don't stay in one place long enough to form lasting attachments.'

'I don't want to give you false hopes, Poppy. I know girls like you want the whole package, but I'm not interested in that right now. I have too many other responsibilities to sort out first before I even think about settling down.'

'That's fine,' Poppy said, even though it wasn't. Could she settle for a short-term fling and leave it at that? How would she feel when it was over? Would she be so deeply in love with him by then her heart would be shattered when he walked out of her life for good?

Wasn't she already a teensy bit in love with him?

He came over and tipped up her chin so his eyes meshed with hers. She had to work hard not to show how conflicted she felt. Emotions she had never felt before were bubbling inside her. It felt like a vicious tug-of-war between pretence and honesty was pulling her in two. She wanted to tell him how she felt, that she loved him and wanted to be with him for ever, but the practical, sensible side of her resisted.

If she told him how she felt he would end their affair before it had even started. At least if she kept her feelings to herself she would have a few precious memories to treasure once he had moved on. And he would move on. Didn't his track record prove it?

'The press will probably hassle you for a few days,' he said. 'Try not to let it get to you.'

'I won't.'

He leaned down and pressed a lingering kiss to her mouth. 'You taste like spun sugar.'

Poppy gave him an arch look. ‘I thought you didn’t have a sweet tooth?’

His dark eyes glinted as he pressed her back down on the bed. ‘I do now,’ he said and covered her mouth with his.

CHAPTER TWELVE

POPPY WOKE TO the sound of birdsong at dawn. She stretched her legs and winced when she felt the tug of her tender feminine muscles. Rafe had been incredibly gentle with her last night, which had made it so much harder for her to keep her emotions in check. She had lain in his arms, feeling satiated, yet strangely dissatisfied. They were so close physically—she seriously wondered if two people could be closer—and yet she felt as if a chasm of difference separated them.

His world was so disparate from hers. He had the money to buy whatever he wanted, wherever he wanted, whenever he wanted. He could travel the globe and not have to stop and count the pennies. He had casual affairs that left no lasting impression on him. He probably didn't even remember their names after a few weeks or months had passed.

Would he remember her after this was over? How long before he forgot her name or what she looked like? How long before someone else took his fancy?

Poppy turned her head and looked at him lying beside her. He was lying on his back, one of his arms loosely around her shoulders, the other hanging over the edge of the bed. His breathing was deep and even, his body relaxed, yet there was a slight frown between his closed eyes, as if his mind was mulling over something complicated.

Before she was even aware she was doing it, she reached up with her fingertip and smoothed away the tiny three-pleat crease.

His eyes opened and met hers. 'Hasn't anyone told you before that you should let sleeping dogs lie?'

She moved her fingertip to his stubbly jaw, tracing a line from the side of his nose to the base of his chin. 'I'm not the least bit scared of dogs, even big scary ones who look like they might bite if cornered.'

He took her finger into his mouth and gently

nipped it with his teeth, his eyes holding hers in a sexy little lock down that made the base of Poppy's spine tingle. 'You'd better stop looking at me like that.'

'How am I looking at you?'

'Like you want me to pin you to the bed and make mad, passionate love to you.'

Poppy felt a frisson of delight pass over her skin. 'Why shouldn't I look at you like that?'

He rolled her onto her back and entangled his legs with hers. 'Because I don't want to make you sore.'

She looked into his espresso-black gaze and felt another shackle around her heart slip away. How could she not love this man? He was so thoughtful and gentle, yet so passionate and attentive. How was she supposed to resist the feelings that were burgeoning inside her?

He was everything she had ever wanted in a partner.

From the first moment his mouth had met hers, she had felt a seismic shift in her body. How would she ever be satisfied with anyone else? Wouldn't she always compare them with him?

His touch was like magic. His kisses were hypnotic, his gaze mesmerising and his possession captivating and cataclysmic. She would never be the same now she had shared this incredible intimacy with him. It wasn't just that he was her first lover; he had touched on something deep inside her that spoke to her on a primal level.

Poppy touched his face again, smoothing away the frown that had appeared again between his brows. 'When I met you for the first time when you came into the shop that day, I thought you were the most arrogant, unfeeling person I had ever met.'

'And now?'

She gave him a little smile that had a hint of reproof about it. 'You're still arrogant.'

He shrugged self-deprecatingly. 'It's my middle name.'

'I kind of figured that.' She trailed her fingertip over his lower lip. 'Are your brothers the same?'

'Raoul less so, Remy more so,' he said, looking at her mouth. 'I guess I fall somewhere in between.'

Poppy felt the rise of his body against her belly.

The roar of his blood incited her own to race frenetically through her veins. Her heart began to thump when she saw the glittering intention in his dark-as-night gaze. Her body gave an involuntary shiver as his mouth came down and covered hers in a kiss that awoke every feminine instinct in her. Her tongue met his in an urgent tangle of lust that made her pelvis throb for his possession. She shifted against him, urging him to complete the erotic dance he had started.

He eased his mouth off hers and went in search of her breasts, trailing his hot, moist tongue over their sensitive peaks in turn. Each roll and glide of his tongue against her flesh escalated her desire. She felt the pull of it between her legs, the pulse of longing that was like a fever building in her blood.

He moved down her body, his mouth a hot, searing trail that made her back arch in delight. He lingered over her belly button, dipping the tip of his tongue into its tiny cave before going lower to where she ached and pulsed with feverish want.

Poppy sucked in a sharp breath as she felt him

stroke her apart. His breath was a warm caress, his touch on her most sensitive point triggering a maelstrom of feeling. He read her body so well, timing the strokes and the pressure until her body responded in a turbulent wave of release that rocketed through her. She clung to the bed with clawing fingers to anchor herself against the avalanche of sensations that shuddered through her body, leaving her spent once it was over.

He stroked his hand down the length of her thigh as he looked into her eyes. 'You're so beautifully responsive.'

Poppy gazed back at him, dazed. She felt stunned by the way he made her feel. Her body was tingling from head to foot, her nerves dancing in delight at what they had experienced under his touch. 'I want to pleasure you,' she said, shyly reaching for him.

He drew in a breath when she curled her hand around his length. She saw the flash of pleasure in his eyes, felt too the rising tension in him as she moved her hand in a rhythmic motion up and down his shaft. She ran her thumb over his moist tip and watched as he fought to control his response. It spurred her on to be even more adventurous. She gave him a sultry look and slithered down his body, breathing over him first, tantalising him with what was to come.

He gripped the sides of her head with his hands. 'If you're not comfortable with doing that…' He let out a short sharp expletive as her tongue found him. 'At least let me put on a condom.'

Poppy pulled back as he fished out a condom. She took the little packet off him and set about putting it on him. He drew in another harsh-sounding breath, his abdomen contracting as she smoothed it over his length. His raw male beauty took her breath away. He was so thick with desire. She could feel the thunder of his blood against her fingers.

She lowered her head to him again, licking him at first, letting him feel the warmth of her tongue through the thin barrier of the condom. She became bolder as her confidence grew, taking him into her mouth, sucking on him with varying degrees of pressure to see what he preferred. He gave her all the encouragement she needed with deep, growly groans of pleasure as the tension built inside him.

It was much more pleasurable than Poppy had been expecting. She had always imagined the act to be a very one-sided affair, and to some degree subservient, perhaps even slightly demeaning.

But it was nothing like that.

The feminine power she had over him thrilled her and excited her. Her lips and mouth registered every subtle change as he hurtled towards the final moment of release. The tension in him rose to a crescendo, his breathing becoming more rapid and uneven, his hands clutching at her head with a desperation that made the blood fizz and sing with delight in her veins. She felt that final cataclysmic explosion; it made the fine hairs on the back of her neck lift up to sense the monumental power of his response to her.

He pulled away from her and dealt with the condom, his breathing sounding ragged in the silence.

'Was that...OK?' Poppy asked.

He cupped one of her cheeks in his hand, his look tender. 'You were wonderful. Perfect.'

'I have a lot of catching up to do,' she said, tracing a fingertip over his collarbone. 'Chloe told me I'd have to have heaps of sex to catch up with other girls my age.'

The smile went out of his eyes and his hand fell away from her face as he got off the bed. 'It's not a competition, Poppy.' He stepped into his trousers and zipped them up almost savagely. 'There's no prize for the person who's bedded the most partners.'

Poppy watched as he shrugged himself back into his shirt. His movements seemed tense, angry almost. 'Do you know how many lovers you've had?'

His frown carved deep into his forehead. 'I stopped counting a long time ago.'

'Have there been any stand-outs?'

He looked at her quizzically. 'Stand-outs?'

'You know...women who've left a lasting impression on you.'

He let out a breath and began to hunt for his shoes. 'No one that springs immediately to mind.'

Not even me? Poppy's heart sank like a stone. She wanted him to see her differently. She didn't want to be just another nameless notch on his bedpost. She wanted to *matter* to him.

To have him love her.

Was it foolish of her to hope he would fall in love with her in spite of the very real differences in their backgrounds? Their physical compatibility was unquestionable, even given her limited experience. She sensed a much deeper connection, one that he might not be ready to admit to, but it was there all the same. Hadn't it been there right from the start? That clock-stopping moment when their eyes had met for the first time when he'd stepped over the threshold of her tearoom. That single moment in time had changed everything. She had thought she was sparring with her worst enemy but instead he had turned into the love of her life.

Their first kiss, the way their mouths had communicated a need that was unlike anything she had felt before; once his mouth had met hers she knew she would never be the same. How could she be? He had unlocked sensations and responses she had not even known she possessed.

Their first time joined together as lovers had

felt much more than a physical union. She had felt as if he had reached deep inside her and touched her soul. She would never be able to look back on their time together as just a casual fling. It wouldn't matter how many times she made love with other partners, she would never forget Rafe's tender touch and mind-blowing passion.

Would he come to think of her the same way?

Poppy swung her legs over the edge of the bed, wincing as her tender inner muscles protested at the movement.

Rafe was beside her in an instant with a frown tugging at his brow. 'Are you all right?'

'I'm fine.'

He slid a gentle hand down the length of her bare arm, encircling her wrist with his fingers.

Poppy looked up into his concerned gaze, her love for him feeling like a clamp around her heart. How was she supposed to navigate her way through an affair with him? She wanted the whole package. She would never be satisfied with a few weeks with him.

She wanted for ever.

She lowered her gaze in case he saw the desperate longing there. 'I'll be fine…'

He brushed her cheek with the back of his knuckles. 'When was the last time you took a break from work?'

'It's been a while…' She frowned as she thought about it for a moment. 'Not since I came back to look after my gran.'

'Can Chloe hold the fort for a few days?'

She met his gaze again. 'How many days?'

He stroked the underside of her chin with a lazy finger. 'Four or five, maybe we could stretch it to a week. I'd have to check my diary.'

'Where are you thinking of going?'

'Paris.'

Poppy's heart swelled in hope. *The city of love…*

'I have a meeting there early next week,' he said. 'But afterwards I thought we could spend a few days doing touristy things. By the time we get back, your house should be fixed.'

Did that mean their affair would be over when they got back? Was this his way of indulging his desire for her without letting her take too permanent a place in his life?

As far as she knew he had never lived with a lover before. But then, strictly speaking, she wasn't living with him. He had offered her a roof over her head until hers was repaired. He wasn't going to make the manor his home. It was a profit-making exercise, a money-spinner that held no sentimental value to him at all.

Poppy rolled her lips together uncertainly. *Could she do it?* Could she step outside of her normal, rather mundane life and spend a few days in his exotic world of untold riches and privilege? 'I'd have to check with Chloe first.'

'Let me know tonight.' He brushed her mouth with a brief kiss. 'I've got to dash. There's a landscaper coming to see me this morning about the gardens. I want to sketch out a few more plans before he gets here.'

Poppy frowned. 'What sort of plans do you have in mind?'

'I want to get rid of the wild garden,' he said. 'It's too rambling and chaotic. I want more structure and formality. It will better suit the overall feel for the hotel I have in mind.'

'But the wild garden is one of the most beautiful features of Dalrymple Manor,' she said. 'How can you possibly think of changing it?'

He gave her the sort of look a parent gives to a child who hasn't quite grasped right from wrong. 'How can you possibly think of leaving it the way it is? It's full of weeds and nondescript plants.'

'Those weeds and nondescript plants have been there for hundreds of years,' she said. 'You can't just waltz in and rip them all out.'

'I can and I will,' he said with a challenging glint of determination in his gaze. 'It's called possession and progress.'

Poppy clenched her jaw and her hands. 'It's called desecration and bad taste.'

His mouth tilted. 'You think I've got bad taste?'

'You have appalling taste.'

He arched a brow. 'In women?'

She gave her head a little toss. 'I definitely think you could lift your standards a bit. That last mistress you had was clearly after money and notoriety. It was pretty obvious she didn't like you as a person; she just liked your money.'

He gave an indifferent shrug. 'She was just another woman who came along.'

'Just like me?'

His gaze held hers for a beat. 'I've not made any promises to you, Poppy.'

'No,' she said, flashing him a defiant look. 'And I'm not making any to you.'

He took that on board with a half-smile that didn't reach his eyes. 'Let me know what you decide about Paris. I'll get my secretary to make the arrangements.'

Poppy let out a jagged breath once he had left. Would she be making the biggest mistake of her life by going with him to Paris? Or would it be an even bigger one to deny herself a precious few days with him before he called an end to their affair?

Rafe tried to give the landscaper his full attention but his mind kept drifting back to Poppy. She had looked so gorgeously tousled this morning after spending the night in his arms. He had watched her sleep for a couple of hours after they had made love. She had curled up against him like a little cat, her soft skin warm and sensual against his.

His stomach gave a little free fall every time he thought of how tender she was after his possession. When he'd disposed of the first condom, he had seen a smear of blood on it. He hadn't thought he would be so moved by the experience of sharing her first time with her. He had thought himself far too modern and progressive to consider a woman's virginity as some sort of prize to gloat over. But the intimacy he had shared with Poppy had made him realise how mundane and predictable his sex life had become over the years. His encounters were little more than physical transactions of mutual pleasure. There was no sentiment attached, no feeling that life would never be the same if that person were never to return to his bed…

'And over here we could do a fountain or water feature.' The landscape designer pointed to the middle of the wild garden. 'We could pave it with sandstone.'

Rafe gave himself a mental shake. 'Right… I'll have a think about it and get back to you.'

'I've had a look at the maze,' the designer said. 'It's going to be a big job to restore it. It's been neglected for years, by the look of it. And that storm the other day didn't help things. It needs replanting in a couple of places.'

'I don't care about the expense,' Rafe said. 'Do what needs to be done.'

'Cute dogs.' The landscape designer crouched down and made 'come here' noises to Chutney, Pickles and Relish who had been following Rafe like devoted slaves since he had walked out of the manor that morning. 'My wife has a couple of Maltese poodly things. Never thought I'd be one to go gaga over a fluffy mutt, but there you go. They worm their way into your heart, don't they?'

'They're not mine,' Rafe said. 'Watch out for the grey and white one. He'll nip at you if you come too close.'

Pickles immediately took shelter behind Rafe's left leg, peering out with his beady gaze. The man straightened after ruffling Chutney and Relish's ears. 'I'll get back to you with a quote on the development and the maze in a day or two,' he said. 'Say hi to Poppy for me.'

Rafe frowned. 'You know her?'

'My mother and her gran were best friends. She's a sweetheart, isn't she? Got a heart of gold. Does a lot for the village—in the background, like. When my wife had a caesarean with our twins, Poppy came by every day with a hot meal prepared. Even took home the washing and brought it back all neatly folded and ironed.' He gave Rafe a man-to-man wink. 'She'll make some lucky guy a fabulous wife one day.'

Rafe stretched his mouth into a tight smile. 'I'm sure she will.'

CHAPTER THIRTEEN

'PARIS…' CHLOE GAVE a wistful sigh. 'You do realise you're living every girl's dream? Being taken to the city of love with a handsome billionaire to be wined and dined and passionately wooed.'

Poppy chewed her lip as she put some pieces of sultana-and-cherry slice on a flowered plate ready for the display cabinet. 'It's mostly a business trip for Rafe. I'm just tagging along as entertainment.'

'I don't believe that,' Chloe said. 'He's falling for you, big time. Next thing you know, he'll be down on bended knee. You see if I'm not right. And what better place to propose to you than Paris?'

'He's not going to propose to me,' Poppy said with a heavy heart. 'He's going to send me on my way once this week in Paris is over with a bit of jewellery as a consolation prize. I bet he won't even choose it himself. He'll get one of his secretaries to do it.'

Chloe sucked in one side of her cheek as she studied Poppy's downcast features. 'You really are in love with him, aren't you?'

Poppy let out a serrated sigh. 'When he came into the shop that first day I thought he was the biggest jerk I'd ever met. It just goes to show you can't trust first impressions. Underneath that cold, hard business front he puts up, I suspect he's a really caring person.'

'So what's the problem?'

Poppy's shoulders dropped. 'He doesn't care about me…or at least, not the way I want him to care.'

'What's the hurry?' Chloe said. 'You've only known him, what, a week or two? Give him time.'

'But what if it's not me he's really after?' Poppy finally voiced the fear that had been lurking in her mind ever since Rafe had made love to her. 'What if he's only involved with me to charm me into selling him the dower house?'

Chloe's forehead wrinkled. 'Do you really think he'd do something as low as that?'

'I don't know… Look at what Oliver did. I didn't see that coming. Maybe I just attract the type of guys who think they can pull the wool over my eyes.'

'You *are* a bit of a babe in the woods,' Chloe said, but not unkindly. 'Be careful, hon. Just take it one day at a time. Enjoy what's on offer while it's on offer. That's all you can do.'

'Do you fly *everywhere* in a private jet?' Poppy asked Rafe the following Monday as they were about to leave London.

'I hate waiting around gate lounges,' he said. 'It's such a waste of time.'

She rolled her eyes at him. 'I hope you realise that, now the dogs have been placed in those plush boarding kennels you organised for them, they'll never be happy staying anywhere else. They'll probably turn their little noses up at their stainless steel dishes when they get back. I'll have to get them gold or silver ones, or maybe diamond-encrusted ones.'

He gave her a bone-melting smile. 'I don't see why they can't have a good time as well as us.'

Poppy had no doubt she was going to have a good time while she was away—a *very* good time. The last few nights with him had left her body tingling with delight. This morning he had joined her in the shower, leaving her quivering with ecstasy. Just looking at him now made her insides slip like a drawer pulled out too quickly. His dark eyes contained a sensual promise that made her toes curl up and her heart race.

There was one attendant on the flight who served them champagne and canapés and then pulled and locked the sliding door across the cabin to give them privacy.

Poppy took a sip of her champagne. 'Do your brothers have private jets too or do you share this one?'

'We each have our own. My grandfather has two.'

She studied him for a moment. 'Do you ever think of how different your life would be if you'd been born into another family? One without loads and loads of money to burn?'

A frown settled between his brows. 'I don't *burn* money for the sake of it, Poppy.'

She toyed with the stem of her glass. 'Maybe not, but I bet you've never had to worry about where your next meal is coming from.'

'I know that anyone looking from the outside would think people with enormous wealth have it easy, but having money brings its own issues,' he said. 'The one you mentioned the first day we met, for instance.'

Poppy screwed up her face as she tried to remember. 'What did I say?'

'You said I probably lie awake at night wondering if people liked me for me or just for my money.'

She pulled at her lower lip with her teeth. 'I probably shouldn't have said that. I didn't even know you then. I was just making horrible assumptions about you.'

He stroked a finger down the back of her hand resting on the armrest between them. 'I made a few about you that weren't all that accurate too.'

Poppy met his gaze. 'I want you to know I like you for you, not for your money. We could've come to Paris by car or even by train or bus and I wouldn't have minded one little bit.'

His smile was lopsided as he brushed the curve of her cheek with an idle fingertip. 'You're very sweet, Poppy Silverton.'

'I expect what you really mean is I'm terribly naïve.'

His smile was exchanged for a frown. 'Why would you think that?'

Poppy gave him a direct look. 'How do I know this trip to Paris isn't part of your plan to get me to relinquish the dower house?'

His frown deepened. 'Is that what you really think?'

'You can't deny you still want it.'

'Of course I still want it,' he said. 'But that's got nothing to do with our affair.'

Poppy wanted to believe him. She *ached* to believe him. But how could she be sure what his motives were? He had been upfront about his intentions over the dower house from the very first day. He wasn't one to be dissuaded from a goal. He played to win, not to lose.

A compromise would be anathema to someone as task-oriented as him. He would see that as failure, as a weakness.

'I'm not going to sell it to you, Rafe. I don't care how many private jets you take me on, or how much champagne you give me to drink. I'm not selling my house to you, or to anyone.'

He unclipped his belt and stood up, raking a hand through his hair in a gesture of frustration and impatience. 'Do you really think I would stoop that low?' he asked. 'What sort of man do you think I am?'

'A very determined one.' She eyeballed him. 'Stealthy, single-minded and steely, or so the press would have us believe.'

He gave a cynical bark of laughter. 'And you take that as gospel, do you?'

'I want to believe your motives are honourable,' Poppy said. 'But how can I be sure you want me for me?'

He came over to her and lifted her chin so her gaze meshed with his. 'I'm not going to deny I want the dower house. I can't go ahead with my development plans for the manor without it. But this thing between us is entirely separate.'

Was it? Was it really?

He unclipped her belt and drew her to her feet. 'I want *you, ma chérie*. I've wanted you from the very first moment I laid eyes on you.'

But for how long? The words were a mocking taunt inside her head. His track record of quickly turned-over relationships didn't bode well for her hopes of marriage and babies and a happy-ever-after. It was the hopeless romantic in her that hoped she would be the one to change him.

How many women just like her had been burnt by the same deluded dream?

Poppy pushed her doubts aside and gave him a little teasing smile as she started working on the knot of his tie. 'So…just how private is this jet of yours?'

His eyes glittered as he tugged her against him. 'Very,' he said and lowered his mouth to hers.

Rafe's apartment was more like a villa than an apartment. It was a six bedroom luxuriously appointed property not far from the Ritz Hotel overlooking *Jardin des Tuileries.* It was definitely the top end of town. For Poppy, who had only ever travelled on a shoe-string budget, it was certainly an eye opener. She tried not to act too star struck or over-awed but it was impossible not to feel a little envious of the wealth Rafe had at his fingertips.

Rafe had organised dinner at Moulin Rouge in Montmartre and Poppy sat transfixed as the can can show Paris was famous for played out so vibrantly and colourfully before her. After the show he took her to another venue where there was live music and dancing.

'But I'm rubbish at dancing,' Poppy protested when he took her by the hand to lead her to the dance floor.

'Just follow my lead,' he said, drawing her close against him.

It was hard at first not to think everyone was looking at her tripping over her own feet, but after a while she started to relax as Rafe led her in a slow waltz to the tune of a romantic ballad.

'See?' he said against her hair. 'You're a natural.'

'You're a very good teacher,' Poppy said, looking up at him.

His pitch-black eyes glinted. 'You're a very fast learner, *ma petite*.'

She moved against him and shivered in delight when she felt his arousal. 'I guess I should make the most of my limited time under your tutelage,' she said flippantly.

His lips pressed together and his eyes lost their light spark. 'We should get going,' he said, dropping his arms from around her. 'It's getting late and I have an early meeting in the morning.'

Poppy mentally kicked herself for spoiling a perfectly good evening. What was the point of reminding him their relationship was temporary? She trudged after him with her spirits sagging like sodden sheets on a clothes line. Why couldn't she just be satisfied with what she had rather than what she didn't have? Most girls would give anything to have a week or two with someone like Rafe. She had seen the envious looks from other women all evening. Rafe's good looks and aura of power and authority were incredibly head-turning. What right did she have to insist on more from him when they had only known each other such a short time?

The problem was she *knew* he was 'the one'. She had known that the first time he had kissed her. His love-making had only reinforced her conviction. She couldn't imagine being with anyone else. She didn't want to be with anyone else.

Once they were out on the street, Poppy touched him on the forearm. 'Rafe, I'm sorry. I'm being a cow. It must be the jet lag.'

His fingers enveloped her hand and gave it a tiny squeeze. 'I understand you want to feel more secure, *mon coeur*. Let's just take it a day at a time, hmm? I have a lot on my mind right now with my work.'

'I'm sorry…I didn't realise,' she said. 'Is your meeting tomorrow worrying you?'

He tucked her arm through his as they walked back to the car. 'There are always worries when you are responsible for people's jobs and careers. Tomorrow's meeting is with one of my accountants based here. For a while now I've had some concerns that he's been fudging the books now and again. I've had an independent audit done. The results will be put on the table tomorrow. It's not looking good.'

'Oh no, that's awful,' Poppy said.

'Yes.' He gave her a brief glance before turning his gaze ahead, resigned. 'I'm not looking forward to it. He's got a wife and young family. He's worked for me since he graduated from university. It's hard not to feel betrayed.'

'There's no worse feeling, is there?' Poppy said. 'That someone you trusted has exploited you.'

He stopped walking and turned to look at her. 'Is that what happened with your boyfriend?'

Poppy grimaced. 'I hate even thinking of him as my boyfriend now. Thank God I didn't sleep with him. I'd have been feeling even more foolish now if I had.'

He tucked a curl of her hair behind her ear, a thoughtful expression on his face. 'I was talking to Howard Compton about you the other day.'

Poppy lifted her brows. 'I didn't know you two were friends.'

He gave her a sheepish smile. 'I drop in every day or so for a wee dram, as he calls it. I can't stand whisky but I haven't got the heart to tell him. I enjoy his company. He's a nice old chap.

Nothing like my grandfather, which is probably why I like him so much.'

'What did you say to him about me?'

'I told him I had drawn up a business plan for you, the one I showed you the other night.'

Poppy bit her lip. She hadn't actually got around to looking at it too closely and she was pretty sure Rafe knew it.

'You have to learn to say no, *ma petite*,' he said. 'You'll go under if you don't learn to stand up for yourself. People will respect you for it.'

'I'll try.'

He looped an arm around her shoulders and, drawing her towards him, kissed the top of her head. 'Good girl.'

Back at his apartment, Rafe came out of the bathroom and found Poppy busily taking pictures of the art deco furnishings with her mobile phone. 'If you like them so much I'll buy you some,' he said.

She swung around guiltily, blushing like a kid caught with her hand in the cookie jar. 'It's a lovely apartment. You have wonderful taste.'

Rafe came over, took the phone out of her hand and tossed it on the bed. 'I want your hands free for the next little while.'

'Oh really?' She gave him a sparkling smile. 'What did you have in mind?'

He unclipped her hair and watched as it tumbled around her shoulders. The honeysuckle fragrance of it wafted towards him. He threaded his fingers through its thick, silky tresses, loving the feel of it against his fingers. He brought his mouth to hers, tasting her sweetness, losing himself in the lush softness of her lips and the shy response of her tongue as he summoned it into play with his.

Her body moved against him in that delightfully instinctive feminine way, fitting against the hard planes of his frame as if she had been tailor-made for him. He put a hand at the base of her spine and pushed her against his erection. His need for her was a throbbing pulse that drove every other thought out of his head. The desire to ravish her was almost overwhelming, but the gentleman in him would not rush her or push her beyond her comfort zone.

She gave a little whimper as he skated a hand over the globe of her breast. He loved the shape of her, the way her breast fit so neatly into his hand, how soft her skin was, how sensitive to his touch.

'You're wearing too many clothes,' he murmured against her mouth.

'So are you.' She tugged his shirt out of his trousers and moved her soft little palm over his chest.

A surge of lust almost knocked him off his feet. He found the zip at the back of her dress and lowered it. Her dress slipped to the floor and she stepped out of the circle of fabric, still with her mouth clamped on his and her slim arms looped around his neck.

Rafe smoothed his hands over her back, deftly unhooking her bra in the process. He slipped off her lacy knickers, running his hands over her neat bottom, teasing her with a feather-light touch on her feminine folds. He felt for her slickness, his insides coiling with desire when he found her ready for him.

She undid his belt and unzipped him with ruthless purpose. He sucked in a breath when she finally uncovered him. Her touch was mind-blowing. The blood roared through his veins, his desire at fever pitch. When she started caressing him in bolder and bolder strokes he thought he was going to disgrace himself.

He pulled her hand away and took a steadying breath. 'Not so fast, *ma belle.*'

'I want you.' Her toffee-brown eyes held his in a sultry little lock that made his heart race. She walked into him until he had nowhere to go but lie on the bed, taking her down with him.

Her body was draped temptingly over him as she took both of his hands and put them above his head. 'What are you doing?' he asked.

'I'm tying you up.'

Rafe laughed as she wrapped his tie around his wrists and anchored it to the bedpost. Did she really think that flimsy piece of silk was going to restrain him? He'd let her play her little game, but he would be free before she could say 'cupcake'. He was the one in control here, not her. But it would be fun to let her think she was on top, so to speak.

She slithered back down his body, her thighs trapping his between hers, the look in her eyes making his blood heat to boiling. She picked up the fullness of her hair and flung it over her shoulder so she could get down to business.

Rafe's insides quivered as she put her lips around him. *No condom.* He tested the hold on the tie but it was surprisingly—*terrifyingly*—firm.

Her first tongue stroke was long, hot, wet and nearly sent him over the edge.

He struggled against the bonds. 'What the hell?'

She looked up from beneath her lashes from where she was poised over his painfully thick erection. 'That's what you get for insisting on a designer brand. You should have settled for a cheap chain-store one.'

Rafe sucked in another breath as she teased him some more with her tongue. He tried to count backwards; he thought of all the distracting things he could, like the mounds of paperwork that needed to be dealt with, but none of it worked. She began to draw on him as if she was going to turn him inside out with the hot, wet suction of her mouth. He felt himself lift off and soar. He lost all sense of himself as he pumped himself into a mindless oblivion that surpassed anything he had felt before.

She gave him a naughty smile as she untied his wrists. 'So, Mr Must Have Control At All Times. How did that feel?'

'Amazing.' Rafe pushed a finger into her and watched as her face gave a spasm of pleasure. She pushed against him, urging him on, inciting him. He withdrew his finger and flipped her around so her back was to him. He pressed up against her, letting her feel the growing, hot, hard heat of him from behind. She gave a sensuous wriggle against him, searching for him with a sexy little hitch of her hips. It was all he could do to stop from thrusting into her without protection. 'Wait,' he said, stalling her with a hand on her left hip. 'I need a condom.'

Once it was on he came back to her, sliding his hands down her slim sides, breathing in the aroused fragrance of her. 'Are you comfortable with this?' he asked against the back of her neck.

She gave a little murmur of assent and wriggled against him again.

Rafe thrust in slowly, gauging her response, trying to keep control when all he wanted to do was explode inside her tight warmth. She urged him on with little kittenish mews that made his skin come up in goose bumps. He started to move, his thrusts going deeper and deeper, then harder and faster. She was with him all the way, her body accepting him, responding to him with such frenzied passion it made him teeter on the edge of control all over again.

He slipped a hand between her legs to give her that extra friction, and within seconds she was convulsing around him, her cries of pleasure and the tight contractions of her body triggering his own spectacular release. He emptied himself, shivering all over in that blissful aftermath.

He didn't want to step away from her and break that intimate connection. He felt his erection subsiding but knew it wouldn't take long to get it going again. His desire for Poppy was increasing rather than abating. Usually by this stage in a relationship he was getting a little restless, even a little bored. But with Poppy every time was so completely different, more exciting, more satisfying…more *addictive.*

Her glib comment about making the most of her time with him had annoyed him. He wasn't ready to commit to anything without some serious thought. Choosing a life partner was a big deal. He had seen too many marriages come unstuck because they had been forged out of lust rather than common sense.

He was a planner, a strategist, not an impulsive fool. He was not at the mercy of his loins.

At least, not unless he was tied up.

His conversation with Raoul had got him thinking, however. He didn't want to end up like his grandfather, having to pay people to be with him in his old age. The thought of a wife who would be a lover, friend and confidante was rather attractive. So too was the thought of children. Only that evening they had walked past a young couple pushing a pram. Rafe had seen Poppy's covert glance at the cute baby inside. It had got him thinking of how beautiful she would look if she were pregnant. With her coltish limbs and ballerina-like figure, she would be all baby. He hadn't realised how sexy a pregnant women looked until now… Or, at least, how sexy Poppy would look.

What are you thinking? You've known her how long—two weeks?

He had to get a grip on himself. Maybe it had been a mistake to bring her to Paris. It wasn't called the city of love for nothing.

Love.

That was one four-letter word he didn't like to think about too much.

Rafe moved away from her and disposed of the condom. She turned and looked at him in that coy way of hers he found so incredibly endearing. She had played the game of temptress with stunning aplomb, but deep down she would always be an old-fashioned girl. He felt a string being plucked deep inside him as she picked up her dress and used it like a shield against her nakedness. 'You don't have to hide yourself from me, Poppy.'

Her teeth bit into her lower lip. 'I know. It's just I can't help thinking you're probably comparing me to all the other women you've slept with.'

The irony was Rafe could barely recall the names, let alone the features, of his previous lovers. He came over to her and cupped her face in his hands. 'You are the most beautiful woman I have ever been with—not just in terms of looks, but in terms of who you are as a person. And let me tell you, that's far more important.'

'Do you really mean that?'

He pressed a lingering kiss to her mouth. 'I mean that.'

CHAPTER FOURTEEN

POPPY WAS WAITING outside the building where Rafe had his meeting when he came out. He had been expecting her to go shopping for the morning. He had even given her a credit card to use. She had slipped it in her purse without argument, but he had seen the way her lips had pressed together momentarily, as if she had felt compromised in some way. Her reaction had been completely different from any other woman he had been with. Some had barely contained their excitement at being given carte blanche. It was a refreshing change to think Poppy had not taken his generosity for granted.

She stepped up and slipped her hand into his. 'Are you OK?'

'I need a drink.'

'That's not always the best solution.'

He pushed a hand through his hair. 'I know. I

hate myself right now. I just sacked a man who has a wife and three little kids.'

She gave him a sympathetic look. 'Was there no alternative?'

Rafe looked down at her heart-shaped face. She was so innocent, so unjaded. 'He's got a gambling problem. He's ripped me off for hundreds of thousands of euros. It's been going on for a couple of years. I should be pressing criminal charges.'

A little worried frown pulled at her brow. 'But you're not going to do that, are you?'

He let out a long, jagged breath. 'No.'

'There are programs, you know? For problem gamblers,' she said. 'What about if you offered to sponsor him through one? You could strike a deal with him. He has to do the program while you support his wife and kids, or he has to go to jail.'

Rafe gripped her by the shoulders and pulling her towards him, pressing a brief, hard kiss to her mouth. 'You are absolutely brilliant. Do you know that?'

She gave him a shy smile. 'I wouldn't go as far as saying that.'

He took out his phone and started scrolling through his contacts. 'Give me five minutes. Once I get this sorted, we are going to have a night to remember.'

It did turn out to be a night to remember, but for all the wrong reasons. Poppy was sitting in an award-winning restaurant with him when Rafe's phone rang. She had seen him switch it to silent as they entered the premises, but even with the subtle background music the vibration of it was still audible. He gave her an apologetic look and took it out of his breast pocket.

His face dropped right in front of her. Her heart contracted in panic as she saw the way his features tightened.

'Is he going to make it?'

Poppy felt her stomach tighten in dread. Whose life was hanging in the balance? Rafe's face was pinched and white with shock. Was it his grandfather; one of his brothers or one of his friends; one of his employees?

'I'll get there as soon as I can.' He ended the call and looked at her, ashen-faced. 'My brother Raoul has had an accident whilst water skiing at Lake Como. He's got suspected spinal injuries.'

'Oh no…'

'I have to go to him.' He got up so abruptly the glasses rattled on the table. 'I'm sorry about this week. I'll have to cut it short. I'll get my Paris secretary to organise your flight home.'

'Can't I come with you?' Poppy asked as they left the restaurant. 'You'll need support and I can—'

'No.' The word was clipped and hard, intractable. 'I want you to fly home. I'll deal with this on my own.'

'But surely it would be better if you—?'

He gave her a frowning glare. 'Did you not hear what I just said? I don't want you with me. This is about my family. It's my responsibility, not yours.'

Poppy flinched. 'I know you're upset, Rafe, but—'

'But what?' he asked. 'You knew this was how it was going to be, Poppy. I never said this was for ever. We both have our own lives. And mine just reared its big, ugly head.'

Her stomach dropped in despair as they made their way back to their hotel in a taxi. What did this mean? Did he mean it was over between them? She wasn't brave enough to ask. She sat in a miserable silence, feeling his tension and worry in the air combining with her own in a knotty tangle that seemed to be pulling on her heart.

When they got back to their hotel, Rafe barely paused long enough to gather his passport and a change of clothes. Poppy felt so helpless. She wanted to reach out to him but it was like an invisible fortress had formed around him. He was closing off from her. She could see it in the tight set of his features, as if something deep inside him was drawing him away from her inch by inch.

'Is there anything I can do?' she asked when she could bear it no longer.

He looked up from his phone after sending another text, one of many he had sent in the last few minutes. 'What?' The one word was sharp and his frown deep, as if he had already forgotten who she was and why she was there.

Poppy felt her heart contract again. 'I said, is there anything I can do for you while you're away?'

'No.' He pocketed his phone, his expression closing off even further. 'There's nothing. I have to do this alone.' He took a short breath and then released it. 'It's over, Poppy.'

'*Over?*' She looked at him numbly. 'You don't really mean that, do you?'

His look was even more distant. 'Look, I have to go. My brother needs me. I'll get Margaret to send you something to make up for this abrupt end to our affair.'

She drew herself up straighter. 'Please don't bother.'

He reached for his jacket. 'I'll be in touch about the dower house. Hopefully we can come to some agreement.'

'I'm not going to change my mind.'

He gave her another grimly determined look. 'Nor am I.'

As he closed the door on his exit, Poppy wondered if he was talking about her, the dower house, or both.

* * *

It was terrible seeing his younger brother in intensive care hooked up to monitoring machines and IV drips. Rafe's stomach was clenched so tightly he could barely breathe. Remy was standing by Raoul's bedside with a look of such bewilderment on his face it reminded Rafe of the day they had been told their parents had been killed. The weight of responsibility back then was like a leaden yoke on his ten-year-old shoulders. He had realised at that moment he had to take control—that at seven and almost nine his brothers were far too young to understand what had happened and how it would impact on them. He'd had to take charge, to step up to the plate and make them feel someone was looking out for them.

He felt the same now.

'He's not going to die.' Rafe said it without really believing it. It was his role to give assurance, to keep control. To support his brothers and keep the family together no matter what tragedy was thrown at them.

Remy swallowed convulsively. 'What if he can't walk again?'

'Don't even think about it,' Rafe said. He had already thought about it—how it would impact on Raoul, who was the most physically active of them all. His brother would rather be dead than spend his life trapped in a wheelchair; Rafe was sure of it. His job now as his older brother would be to keep him focused on getting as well as he could, to give him hope that he would one day be able to walk again. Medical breakthroughs were happening all the time, admittedly not as quickly as everyone hoped, but it would be crazy to give up hope. He had to keep Raoul positive about a possible recovery.

He looked at his brother lying so pale and broken. He looked at those long, strong legs lying useless in the hospital bed. How would Raoul cope with never feeling the floor beneath his feet, the sand between his toes…the sensuous feel of a lover's legs entwined with his?

It was painfully, torturously ironic that only days ago Raoul had expressed to Rafe over that beer they had shared his desire to settle down. How likely was that going to be now? What if he had no function at all? The doctors had been very cautious in what they had said so far. Perhaps they didn't know until more scans and tests were done. Spinal injuries could be mild or serious and just about everything in between.

'We'll have to tell *Nonno,*' Remy said, pulling Rafe out of his painful reverie.

'Yes.' Rafe stood up and took out his phone. 'He won't be much help, though. He'll just blame Raoul for being such an adrenalin-junkie. You were probably too young to remember what he said when *Mama* and *Papa* were killed. But I have never forgotten and I've never forgiven him.'

'I remember…' Remy's expression was shadowed, haunted. He swallowed again, thickly, as if something hard and misshapen was stuck in his throat. 'Did you know Raoul was thinking about getting engaged to Clarissa Moncrief? I think he was going to propose to her while they were on this trip to the lake.'

Rafe felt his stomach clench again. He had caught a glimpse of Clarissa in the waiting room earlier. She had darted out to the ladies' room rather than speak to him. That didn't bode well in his opinion. Would she stick around for Raoul if things didn't go according to plan?

He couldn't help thinking of Poppy, how she had offered to come with him to support him. He had pushed her away because that was what he always did when he had to focus.

He missed her.

It was hard to admit it, but he did. He missed her in a hundred different ways—her smile her tinkling-bell laugh; the scent of her, a mixture of sugar and spice and all things nice.

But he would damn well have to get used to missing her. He couldn't take her with him back to Italy once this was sorted out. It had been crazy to think of a future with her, or a future with anyone right now. He had even more responsibilities on his shoulders now. How could he possibly think of settling down when Raoul was in such a state? It would be selfish and crass of him to rub his brother's nose in it by announcing his own engagement.

But you love her, you idiot.

Hang on a minute. His sensible control-centre

cut in. What fool would fall in love so quickly? It was lust, that was what it was.

He should never have got into an affair with her in the first place. He'd been blindsided by lust. It had affected his judgement. It was uncharacteristic of him to act so impulsively and now he had to deal with the consequences. She would find someone else, someone who was more in her world of hearth and home and cute, fluffy dogs.

But the least he could do was go and see her about the dower house once he got Raoul stabilised.

That was the plan, the goal.

Now he had to focus.

'I know you told me never to mention his name around here again,' Chloe said a couple of weeks later. 'But have you heard how Rafe's brother doing? There's been nothing in the press since the first report of the accident. It's like there's been a block out on it or something.'

Poppy let out a painful sigh. 'I called his secretary a couple of times. There's still some uncertainty about his mobility. He has some feeling in his legs, so at least that's a positive. It could be much worse.'

'God, life really sucks sometimes,' Chloe said. 'Is Rafe coming back to the manor? Did his secretary say anything about his plans?'

'She said he would be back in a couple of weeks to pick up his things.'

'Don't give up on him yet,' Chloe said. 'Sometimes tragic occurrences make people take stock of their lives. He might want you with him by his side as he helps his brother get through this.'

Poppy wished she had Chloe's confidence but she knew Rafe was a lone wolf when it came to handling difficult things. It had taken a lot for him to tell her about his concerns with the accountant who had been defrauding him. He had told her even less about his childhood, but she suspected it had been desperately lonely, and that he had been given far too much responsibility for a ten-year-old boy when his parents had died. It had left its mark on him. He was used to dealing with things on his own. He didn't want anyone to see the heavy toll it took on him.

Wasn't that why he had pushed her away?

He felt responsible for his family. He wasn't used to sharing that with anyone.

He worked ridiculously punishing hours to keep his and the family's business at the top of its game. She sensed his inner drive was not so much about a desire to be super-successful, but more to compensate for the emptiness he felt at being left an orphan so young.

Was it too much to hope that he would one day see that he didn't have to do it on his own? That he could share the load with someone who cared about him and his happiness?

Of course it was.

She couldn't go on with this idealistic way of viewing the world that everything would turn out in the end. Life was hard at times and she had to be hard to cope with it.

It was time to toughen up.

CHAPTER FIFTEEN

RAFE DROVE DOWN to the manor three weeks later. He had a pounding headache; he was tired from not having slept properly since he had found out about his brother's accident. Raoul was a lot better physically—the concussion he'd sustained had gone and his right arm that had been broken was healing well—but it was obvious he was having difficulty accepting his spinal injury. He'd had surgery to decompress the spine but the doctors were still a little cagey about how good his overall recovery would be.

When Rafe had left the private rehab unit Raoul had been transferred to, his brother had been sitting in his chair staring blankly out of the window. He had barely spoken a word since he'd left the hospital. It was devastating to witness. Rafe couldn't bear to see his vibrant brother slumped so sullenly and listlessly in that wretched chair.

Rafe blamed Clarissa Moncrief. Raoul had proposed the night before the accident and she had readily accepted. Rafe didn't believe for a second she loved Raoul or that Raoul had loved her, but that wasn't the point. She had ended their engagement with a chilling disregard for his feelings.

Rafe was determined to get Raoul out of this slump of self-pity. He was in the process of tracking down a specialist he'd read about in an article online, a young English woman called Lily Archer who had worked with the young daughter of a wealthy sheikh who had suffered a horse riding accident. Halimah Al-Balawi had made a stunning recovery that had defied the doctors' prognosis. Rafe was determined to engage Miss Archer's services no matter what it cost and no matter what resistance his brother put up. Raoul could be stubborn when things didn't go his way, but Rafe had a gut feeling Lily Archer was just the person to sort him out.

But before Rafe went back to be with Raoul he had one other thing to sort out. He hadn't heard from Poppy, but then he hadn't expected to. He had made things pretty clear to her. But it niggled at him that he could have handled things a little better. He had been caught off-guard in Paris. He had shut down as soon as he'd heard about his brother's accident. It was how he always handled things, by closing off all distractions and concentrating on the task at hand.

But seeing how Clarissa had walked so callously out of his brother's life had pulled him up short. He hadn't liked what he had seen when he examined himself. How had Poppy felt to be dismissed like that? How could he have done that to her?

The lights were on in the dower house as he pulled up. He saw Poppy moving about the kitchen as he walked up the path to the back door. She was wearing her flowery apron and her hair was tied up on top of her head. There was a streak of flour over one cheek as she carried a tray of something to the oven.

The dogs must have heard him, as they started their maniacal barking, and Poppy immediately stiffened, put the tray back down on the bench and turned to see him through the window near the back door. Her face turned as white as the flour on her cheek, but then she seemed to compose herself. Her mouth tightened as she took off her oven mitts and, placing them on the counter, came over to open the door. 'Yes?'

Rafe knew he deserved a cool welcome but this wasn't like the Poppy he knew. 'Hi. I saw your light on.'

'I do that after dark,' she said. 'It's expensive, but I'm covering all my costs now that I'm following your business plan. No more freebies. No more credit. No more being taken advantage of. Wish I'd done it earlier.'

Rafe gave her a twisted smile. 'Good for you.'

She was like a stranger, a cold, distant stranger who didn't smile, whose toffee-brown eyes didn't light up when she saw him. Even the dogs seemed to sense the change, for they were not jumping around him vying for his attention but standing well back, eyeing him suspiciously. Pickles was giving him that beady look again, as if to say, "I knew I couldn't trust you".

'I should've called to tell you I was coming,' Rafe said.

'Why?' She gave him a hardened look. 'So I could roll out the red carpet for you?'

He frowned. 'No, it's just that I wanted to explain why I left you in Paris like that.'

'You don't need to explain it. I totally got it, Rafe. You didn't need me any more. You wanted to be on your own so you could concentrate on your brother. How is he?'

'He's out of hospital,' he said. 'I'm hoping to take him to his villa in Normandy once he's cleared from rehab.'

'There's been nothing in the press.'

'No, we've been trying to keep things pretty quiet. But I'm not sure how long that will last.'

A silence chugged past.

Rafe couldn't believe how hard this was. He had been expecting… What had he been expecting? He felt out of his depth, out of balance, disoriented. She was so unreachable, so tightly contained, he felt like an invisible wall was around her.

'I've come to a decision,' Poppy said. 'You can buy the dower house. I don't want it any more.

It should never have been separated from the manor. They belong together.'

Rafe blinked to reorient himself. 'How much do you want?'

'Twenty-five percent above market value.'

He let out a slowly measured breath. 'You drive a hard bargain.'

'I had a very good teacher.'

He searched her features for any sign of a chink in that shiny new armour but she was as hard as nails. He felt a sinkhole of sadness open up inside him. She'd had a very good teacher indeed.

He had done that to her.

'I'll get my secretary to tee things up,' he said.

'Fine.'

There was another clunky silence.

'Is there anything else?' Her tone was impatient and unfriendly. Rafe recognised it, for he had used it a thousand times when he had wanted to dismiss someone who was taking up too much of his precious time.

'No.' He gave her a tight, formal smile. 'That's about it.'

She didn't return his smile. She didn't even

wait until he'd turned his back to go back down the path before she shut the door.

Rafe stared at the wood panelling for a moment. He toyed with the idea of knocking and starting over, but he dismissed the thought before it took hold.

It was better this way. He'd got what he wanted; she was selling him the dower house.

Goal.

Focus.

Win.

But it was ironic that the victory, now he had it, didn't taste so sweet.

'Any luck on tracking down that rehab woman Lily Archer?' Rafe asked his secretary when he got back to London after he'd taken Raoul to his villa in Normandy.

'Yes, but apparently she doesn't work with male clients,' Margaret said.

Rafe exhaled in irritation. 'Then get her to change her mind. I don't care how much it costs.'

'How is Raoul?'

'The same.' He scraped a hand through his hair.

'Won't eat. Barely drinks. Just sits there brooding all the time.'

'A bit like you, then.'

Rafe's brows snapped together. 'What's that supposed to mean?'

Margaret gave him a knowing look. 'You remind me of one of my sons. He's an all-or-nothing thinker. He doesn't know how to compromise. It doesn't have to be either-or, Rafe. You can help Raoul and be happy in your love life.'

'I don't have a love life.' He strode over to the window and looked at the dismal weather outside.

'You miss her, don't you?'

Rafe swung back to glower at her. 'You might want to have another look at your job description. As far I as recall, it says nothing about you making comments on my private life.'

'You're a good boss, Rafe, and you're a good man,' Margaret said. 'What you've done for Armand, your accountant in Paris, is proof of that.'

'That was Poppy's idea, not mine.' He thrust his hands in his pockets, still scowling. 'I was going to send him to rot in prison.'

'No, you weren't,' Margaret said. 'You'd have

found a way to help him. Just like you help lots of people. Like that foundation you set up for kids who've lost their parents. Funny how the press like to report on who you're sleeping with but they never report on all the good things you do.'

Rafe turned back to the window. He couldn't bear the thought of sleeping with anyone but Poppy. His need for her was an ache that had settled around his heart like a set of ten-kilogram dumb-bells. Every breath he took felt painful. It wasn't just the sex he missed, which was ironic, because that in itself was way out of character for him.

It was her smile he missed, the way her gorgeous brown eyes lit up whenever she saw him. The way her touch soothed the wound of loneliness inside him that he had not even realised he'd possessed until she had eased it. The way she gave herself to him with such complete trust.

But he had destroyed the things he loved most about her. She didn't look at him like that any more. She didn't want to touch him. She didn't trust him.

Could he win back her trust? Could he make her smile at him? Could he make her eyes sparkle with delight when he walked into the room?

'Do you want me to send Miss Silverton some jewellery?' Margaret asked. 'Rubies, sapphires or maybe pearls? They'd look rather nice with her colouring, don't you think?'

Rafe turned and faced her. 'No, I'll do it myself.'

Margaret's pencilled brows rose above the frame of her tortoiseshell glasses. 'Are you sure?'

'Absolutely.'

Rafe had never been surer of anything in his life. It was like a stone curtain had lifted in his brain. 'Cancel all of my appointments,' he said. 'I'm heading out of town.'

'Do you need me to book a hotel for you?'

'No, I'm going to stay at the manor.'

'But I thought you were going to sell it.' She swung around in her chair to look at him as he reached for his jacket. 'You told me to contact the agent about putting it back on the market.'

'Sell it? Are you crazy?' He snatched up his keys off the desk. 'I'm going to live there.'

* * *

Poppy was emptying the display cabinet at the end of the day when the doorbell chimed. A shiver rose over her skin and her heart started to gallop. She slowly turned around and her breath caught in her throat. Rafe was standing there, looking as gorgeous as ever, if a little tired. There were shadows beneath his eyes and his face looked a little drawn, as if he'd lost weight.

She put on her business face, but it hurt to keep it there. He looked *so* worn out. She had to control the impulse to reach out to him and give him a hug. 'Would you like a coffee?'

'Actually, what I'd really like is a cup of tea.'

She blinked. 'Tea?'

He gave her a wry smile. 'The hospital coffee was awful. It was even worse at the rehab centre. I had to resort to tea; I got used to it after a while. Now I can't get through the day without a cup or two.'

'I never thought I'd see the day,' Poppy said with forced lightness. 'I don't suppose you'd like a piece of cake?'

'Do you have any butter cake?'

She blinked again. 'Butter cake?'

'Preferably raw.'

Her eyes almost popped. '*Raw?*'

He smiled again but there was hint of wistfulness about it. 'My mother used to bake for us. She didn't want us to grow up with cooks and housekeepers doing everything for us. My favourite cake was vanilla butter-cake. She always used to let me lick the bowl. The day before she and my father were killed, she'd baked one and gave me a spoonful of the batter.'

Poppy blinked again but this time to hold back her tears. 'Oh Rafe…'

'I guess it would be quite a novel thing, having a raw wedding cake,' he said. 'Do you think anyone's ever done that before?'

Poppy's heart sank. 'You're getting married?'

His dark eyes twinkled. 'I hope to very soon.'

She swallowed a tight lump in her throat. She could barely look at him in case he saw the bitter disappointment in her eyes. 'Who's the lucky girl?'

Rafe took her hands in his. 'That's what I love about you, Poppy. You take nothing for granted.

You're modest and gracious and so incredibly sweet, I can't bear the thought of spending another day without you.'

Her eyes were so wide they looked like satellite dishes. 'You love me?'

'I think I fell in love with you the first day I walked in here and met your beautiful eyes. I loved your feistiness, the fact that you were so completely undaunted by me. You were prepared to fight for what you believed in. But what I admire even more about you is how you put your own needs aside for others. The way you realised the manor and the dower house belong together. I was too stubborn to see that but, even though you wanted to keep your house, you saw the greater good in letting it go.'

'I can't believe I'm hearing this…'

Rafe smiled as he drew her closer. 'Marry me, *ma petite*. Please?'

Her dimpled smile was the most beautiful thing he had ever seen. 'Yes.'

He could not believe how one simple word could make him so happy. 'I have something for you,' he said, taking out a velvet box from his jacket pocket. 'I had it designed specially.'

Poppy held her breath as he opened the box to reveal a princess-cut diamond that glittered brilliantly. 'It's so beautiful…'

He took it out and slipped it on her finger, holding her hand in his. 'Diamonds are for ever, *ma cherie*. I won't settle for anything less from you. I hope you realise that. And I want babies. At least two.'

She gave him a smile that made her eyes dance. 'I love you.'

He gathered her close. 'I love you so much. I can't believe I didn't realise it earlier. I must have hurt you so much by leaving you in Paris like that—and then when I came to see you at the dower house. I was so shocked in the change in you. I thought I'd lost you for ever, that I'd changed you for ever.'

Poppy rested her head against his chest. It was the most wonderful feeling in the world to belong to someone who loved her. She felt it in his touch, in his gaze, in the strong, protective shelter of his arms. 'It was so hard to be like that with you. I'm surprised you didn't see through it. I was sure you would call my bluff. But you're here now, that's all that matters.'

He lifted her face to press a lingering kiss to her mouth. 'How do you feel about living at the manor?'

Her face lit up with excitement. 'Do you mean it?'

He smiled down at her. 'It'd be a perfect home for a family, don't you think?'

She threw her arms around him and hugged him tightly. 'It would be a dream come true.'

* * * * *

Mills & Boon® Large Print

January 2014

CHALLENGING DANTE
Lynne Graham

CAPTIVATED BY HER INNOCENCE
Kim Lawrence

LOST TO THE DESERT WARRIOR
Sarah Morgan

HIS UNEXPECTED LEGACY
Chantelle Shaw

NEVER SAY NO TO A CAFFARELLI
Melanie Milburne

HIS RING IS NOT ENOUGH
Maisey Yates

A REPUTATION TO UPHOLD
Victoria Parker

BOUND BY A BABY
Kate Hardy

IN THE LINE OF DUTY
Ami Weaver

PATCHWORK FAMILY IN THE OUTBACK
Soraya Lane

THE REBOUND GUY
Fiona Harper

Mills & Boon® Large Print

February 2014

THE GREEK'S MARRIAGE BARGAIN
Sharon Kendrick

AN ENTICING DEBT TO PAY
Annie West

THE PLAYBOY OF PUERTO BANÚS
Carol Marinelli

MARRIAGE MADE OF SECRETS
Maya Blake

NEVER UNDERESTIMATE A CAFFARELLI
Melanie Milburne

THE DIVORCE PARTY
Jennifer Hayward

A HINT OF SCANDAL
Tara Pammi

SINGLE DAD'S CHRISTMAS MIRACLE
Susan Meier

SNOWBOUND WITH THE SOLDIER
Jennifer Faye

THE REDEMPTION OF RICO D'ANGELO
Michelle Douglas

BLAME IT ON THE CHAMPAGNE
Nina Harrington

0114 Rom LP